HER
FRACTURED
BUTTERFLY

DEANN F. JONES

Contents

Triggers

Dear reader,

Thank you for picking up *Her Fractured Butterfly*. Before you dive into Daria and John's story, I want to take a moment to address the sensitive nature of some of the themes explored within these pages.

This novel delves deeply into the complexities of trauma, healing, and resilience, but it does so through experiences that may trigger some readers. Topics such as abuse, addiction, mental health struggles, and self-discovery are integral to the characters' journeys. The elements portrayed aim to reflect the realities many face while showcasing the hope and strength that can arise from difficult situations.

I believe storytelling is a powerful way to connect, understand, and even heal. But I also understand that some subjects may be challenging to read, even in a fictional setting. Your mental well-being is important, so please approach this story with caution and care if these topics are close to your heart.

To help readers make informed decisions, here is a list of potential triggers present in *Her Fractured Butterfly*:

1. **Childhood trauma**

2. **Physical abuse**

3. **Emotional abuse**

4. **Sexual abuse/activity (explicit)**

5. **Abandonment issues**

6. **Addiction and substance abuse**

7. **Mental health struggles, including anxiety and PTSD**

8. **Nightmares and flashbacks**

9. **Violence**

10. **Self-doubt and feelings of worthlessness**

11. **Gaslighting and manipulation**

12. **Grief and loss**

13. **Parental neglect**

14. **References to suicide (non-explicit)**

Thank you for trusting me with your time and attention.

With gratitude and understanding,

DeAnn F. Jones

Chapter One

Home Again

(2021)

Daria arrived at the LBA airport after a long flight. She was feeling a mix of excitement and trepidation as she stepped off the plane and took her first breath of English air in almost twenty years. She was eager to return to the UK, this familiar place she used to call home. As she settled into her seat on the shuttle bus, Daria's thoughts turned to her great-uncle's house. *Will anyone still live there? Will anyone still be alive?* She was concerned because the phone numbers she had given to the police officer years ago were disconnected.

Her heart pounded as she walked to the door of the terrace home where she used to live. She stood, debating whether to knock, when the door opened. She recognized the face right away. It was her great-aunt, Minnie. "Auntie?"

"Who, dear?" The woman cupped her ear.

Figuring she may be hard of hearing, she spoke louder. "Aunt Minnie, it's me, Daria."

"Daria?" Minnie looked hard at Daria's face and then touched her cheek with recognition. "Oh! You've come home! Come in, come in."

Daria entered the house and found that very little had changed since she left. She followed her great-aunt to the kitchen and declined her offer to put the kettle on, instead asking her to sit. "Auntie, how have you been?"

With a shaky voice. "I'm just a lonely old widow now. I don't usually get many visitors these days."

"I'm so sorry, Auntie. What about Grandpa?"

"Oh dear, he was heartbroken after you left. The only thing that kept him going were your letters."

Letters? What letters? One more mystery to unravel ... did Uncle write them? He must've to keep them from looking for me ...

"He missed you so. We were all sorry that you couldn't make the funeral."

Through her tears, she thought better of trying to tell her elderly aunt the whole truth, so she asked about Jet's parents.

"Oh, his father is still alive, but his mother died shortly after John married a few years ago."

Her heart sank. *Married? You knew it was a possibility. Why are you so shocked?* "I'm so sorry it took me so long to visit Auntie. But I'm here now if you need anything."

"I was just on my way out when you stopped by to get some groceries."

"I can get them for you. Do you have a list?"

"Oh, that would be so kind of you. My legs just aren't what they used to be."

"Perfect, let me take that on for you. I'm here now, so I can get your groceries for you from now on. Would you like that?"

"That's so sweet of you, dear."

Daria grabbed her list and headed to the local store. While walking down one of the aisles, she noticed a woman stretching to reach a can on the top shelf. Daria empathized with her situation because she understood the struggles of being on the shorter side.

The woman moved the item precariously close to the edge, but as she tried to grab it, the can tipped over and fell to the ground. "Oh frick n frack, n frack n frick!" The woman exclaimed in a whispered voice.

It was Penny's little sister. Daria didn't recognize her at first, but the familiar phrase the woman used when she was frustrated brought a smile to her face. Daria snickered quietly as she watched the woman kneel to pick up the can she'd dropped.

"I'm sorry," Daria said, her voice tinged with amusement. "It's been a long time since I heard someone say that."

The woman glanced up at her, looking apologetic. "Yeah, it's kind of my way of not cursing in public. I thought I was the only one who said that."

Daria chuckled. "Unless your name is Catherine, I think someone else is using it too."

The woman's expression turned serious. "How do you know my name?"

Now it was Daria's turn to look serious. "Do you have a sister named Penny?"

"Yes," the woman replied cautiously.

Daria's face lit up with recognition. "Oh my goodness, Catherine, you sure have grown up. Well—we all have, I guess. I'm Daria—we used to have sleepovers, remember? How are you?"

Catherine squinted as she looked more closely at Daria, realization dawning. "Yeah, yeah, I see it now. Lily?"

Daria hesitated before responding, "Uhhh, yeah ... no one's called me that in years. I've been away for so long, I didn't recognize you. I just got back into town."

Catherine crossed her arms, scrutinizing Daria with a mix of disbelief and suspicion. "I can't believe it—the girl who broke Jet's heart!"

Daria forced a smile, though the grief was evident in her voice. "Yeah, that was a long time ago..."

An awkward silence hung between them as Catherine continued to scrutinize her, still trying to process the shock. She shook her head, clearly unsettled. "I still can't believe it's you. What happened? You just disappeared, and Jet was a mess. You didn't even say goodbye."

Daria shifted uncomfortably, the weight of old memories pressing down on her. She glanced around, as if searching for an escape route. "Yeah, it got complicated. Life took some unexpected turns. I never intended to leave like that."

Catherine softened, her curiosity giving way to concern. "I guess ... It must have been tough."

Daria nodded, her voice barely above a whisper. "It was."

Glancing at her watch, Daria seized the opportunity to leave. "Oh, hey, I have to run—just picking up groceries for my aunt. But it's good to see you again. We'll have to catch up sometime!"

With that, Daria offered a quick wave and hurried off, her heart racing. She couldn't get out of there fast enough. Catherine stood in the middle of the aisle, still processing the encounter, as Daria rushed away. At the counter, Daria fumbled with her wallet, paid for her items, and left the store in a haze, her mind reeling from the unexpected reunion.

Back at the hotel, Daria sat on the bed, feeling lost and uncertain about what to do with herself now that Jet was married. She understood that chasing after him was not an option, and she couldn't blame him for getting married. After all, she had been married, too, in a way.

Still, her heart shattered with a painful ache as she thought about the man she had to leave behind—again. It was time to accept her reality and move on. She closed her eyes, recalling the bittersweet memories of their love—the feel of his touch, the scent of his cologne lingering in the air, and the echo of his laughter. She tried to convince herself that she had been fortunate to experience such a profound love at least once in her life, and she should be grateful for it.

So, with a heavy heart, she once again decided that it was time, once and for all, to let go and move forward, even though it was easier said than done.

"But now what? Torn between her reluctance to return to the farm and the hesitation of leaving the only family she had left, Daria also couldn't bear the thought of running into him if their paths were to cross. And that meant staying in town was not an option. The UK was her true home, or at least it's what felt like home. Weighing her options, she wanted to find somewhere nearby but secluded.

It was settled. Daria needed a means of transportation to commute to visit her great-aunt weekly, so she splurged with some of the money the kids gave her.

She found an old, solid black 1970 Dodge Challenger that had been restored. After cranking it up and hearing the roar of good ole American muscle, she bought it and affectionately named it 'The Beast'.

It still had a left-side drive, but she could handle the conversion. She drove it out into the countryside, looking for just the right place, when she came across a small village with cobblestone buildings and roads.

The village was quaint, exuding all the old-world charm one would expect from a medieval setting, but modernized just enough to house independent family-owned shops and cafes for today's tourists.

Nestled on rolling hills with beautiful views of the moorland, one could easily conjure scenes from Gothic romance novels of the past. The blending of historical esthetics with contemporary conveniences created an inviting atmosphere that resonated with Daria.

Mainly pedestrian streets rested between the buildings, and after she spent the afternoon wandering through the village, she walked back to the Beast and headed out.

She pulled into a pub just past the cobblestone roads and onto the blacktop. The large car park was gravel as she crunched to a stop. She needed to rest, eat, and maybe try to get a feel for the people of this community.

Walking in from the entrance of the pub, she found herself in a spacious bar area with an inviting atmosphere. Black leather couch-like benches and circular tables lined one wall, and a couple of wide booths sat on the other, offering ample seating for patrons.

Since it was a weekday, it wasn't crowded, so she found a quiet corner and sat down to decide what to order. After studying the menu, she stood, took a deep breath, and looked around the room again, absorbing the place's ambiance.

This pub had a unique aura compared to the pubs of her past, although the furniture and decor were similar. She couldn't quite pinpoint the exact feeling she was getting. Was it just comfortable? Or was it something else? Whatever it was, she thought, it didn't matter. What truly mattered was that it felt right—as if she was supposed to be there.

She made her way to the bar. Placed her order and met a jolly-looking fellow, probably in his early sixties. He had bright green eyes and a thick head of short black curls and only a sprinkling of gray framing his face.

He spoke with a strong Irish brogue and stood around five foot ten. She noticed his large belly straining the buttons on his too-small shirt through his apron.

His name was Sullivan, Sully for short, and the place was his. He gave her a bright grin and asked, "What can I getcha, lass?"

"What's your specialty?"

"Oh now, dhat would be me wife's Irish stew, but we only serve it to our special guests." He looked her up and down with one eye closed and said, "You look pretty special to me, lass."

She smiled and sat at the bar. "Well, thank you for that. I haven't been special in a long time."

"Oh, now that can't be, a fine lass such as yourself."

"No, it's true. I've been living on a farm for the last almost twenty years. Finally made it home again."

"Well, den, I guess we be needing a homecoming drink to boot?" And he sat a two-finger pour of bourbon in front of her.

She took a sip. "Ohhhh, that's nice."

"So, ye know your bourbons?"

"Just the good ones. I lived in Kentucky."

"Aye, but do dey compare to an Irish whesky?"

"Well, I think it depends on what you're chasing. Do you want it smooth and light with a hint of sweetness or richer with vanilla or caramel notes?"

Sully was impressed. They sat talking about liquor and the local fare for what seemed like hours while she ate. It was getting late, and they were the only two left in the pub besides his wife, who came in to remind him of it.

"Well, thank you, Sully; I've thoroughly enjoyed this evening. You have a lovely place here."

"Well, don't ye be leavin' town without comin' back to see us, lass."

"I'll be sure of it. Goodnight." She left and got to her car, then remembered she had not made arrangements for a room.

She hadn't planned on staying the night, but now it was late. *Guess I'm bunking in the car tonight.* She locked the doors, grabbed her coat for a pillow, lifted the armrest, and settled in for the night.

A short while later, just as she was nodding off, she heard a tapping on the window. And then a flash of light in her face.

"Oi, lady, ye can't sleep 'ere!"

She sat up, half asleep. "What?"

"Ye can't sleep here; ye gotta go home."

About that time, Sully and his wife were walking out to leave for the evening. "Oi, Sully, des girl's pissed in your park. Should I take 'er in?" Sully walked over and saw Daria.

She was wide awake at this point. "I'm not drunk. Would you stop pointing that thing in my eyes, please?" Now, irritated. She opened the door and got out.

"What's de matter, lass? Did ye car break down?"

"No, I'm sorry. It's all my fault, Sully. I spent so long in the pub I completely forgot to make arrangements for a room tonight. I figured I would just sleep in my car and find something in the morning. But this guy—"

"I'll not hear of such a ting. Get ye tings, lass, and come wet me. Rory, go home; she's staying 'ere tonight."

"No, honestly, I'll be fine out here."

His wife, Fi, said, "No use arguing deary, once he's made his mind up."

Daria grabbed her bag and coat and walked back into the pub with Sully and Fi. "Now, it's not much, but it's warm, and dere's a kettle in de ketchen for in de morning. I'll be back 'round noon."

His wife took Daria's arm and led her into the office area. "You make yourself at home, deary."

They showed her the office with a couch and a private bathroom, then Fi pulled out a blanket from the closet and gave it to her. "Sully, this is too much."

"Now, now, lass, I'll not hear another word; besides, des ensures us another visit with ye."

"You're very kind. Thank you both very much."

"Alright now, we'll be seein' ya in de morning."

"Goodnight." They locked up and left.

Daria had a comfortable night's sleep on the small couch, and the following morning, she woke up early and explored the main pub.

The building itself was a large, stand-alone structure, and she couldn't help but notice that it seemed to be the main house of a long-forgotten country home. But what really caught her eye was the main stone wall, which featured a massive floor-to-ceiling fireplace that must have been used for cooking during an era long gone.

Standing beside the bar, she found the long, galley-style kitchen at the rear of the building. It seemed to be well-equipped, and it reminded her of Sully's invitation to start the kettle. The place was a perfect blend of rustic charm and modern amenities, and she couldn't wait to explore it further. But first, tea!

After sipping her first cup of morning brew, she took it upon herself to clean the pub area. Not that it wasn't tidy, but she had her own level of cleanliness, and she wanted to repay their hospitality. Then, remembering Sully's vision for his back-bar area during their conversation, she arranged the liquor and fixed the lighting. It was only a loose wire and easily repaired.

Finished with her tasks, she got the kettle going again, then settled in and waited for Sully and his wife.

Promptly at noon, they arrived at a fresh-smelling pub. Sully immediately noticed the lighting behind the bar. "What's all des?"

"I just wanted to repay you for your kindness last night."

"Not necessary at all, lass. But how did ye—"

"Lived on a farm for almost twenty years, remember?" She smiled and winked at him. "You learn many trades."

"Oh, lass, it looks wonderful!" He walked over and hugged her with one arm as he stared at the bar. "You're hired!" He joked.

"You're welcome."

"I'm serious. Would ya be lookin' for a job, by any chance?"

"Well, actually, I am. I've been looking for a little place to settle, and this place has definitely caught my eye."

"Well, dhat settles it. We need de help, especially on de weekends now, dhat tourist season is coming."

"Sounds like a plan; know any affordable rooms for rent?"

"Well, de one you stayed in last night's available; we could fex it up a little, make it nice. I'll not be needin' it as an office, and dere's a private bathroom; you're welcome to de ketchen anytime, and ded I mention it's free."

"Sully, I'm a total stranger. Are you sure?"

"Lass, if ye were gonna rob me blind, ye coulda done it last night. Instead, I came into a clean pub and fexed lightin' dhat saved me money. It's yours."

Her eyes watered as she nodded. "Thank you, Sully; you won't regret this."

Chapter Two

New Girl

(2021)

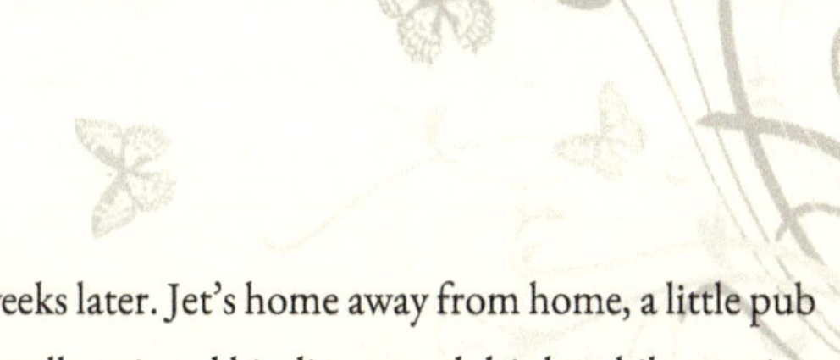

It was a Wednesday night several weeks later. Jet's home away from home, a little pub called Sully's. A quiet spot where he usually enjoyed his dinner and drinks while meeting up with some of the locals.

He and his bandmate, Ronny, were back in town for some rest and relaxation and heard a rumor about a new girl causing quite a stir in this sleepy little village.

Expecting a crowded pub, Jet and Ronny discreetly took a seat away from the bar to see what the excitement was about.

Sully was mingling, greeting the guests, when he noticed the two men sitting at a table in the corner. He walked over and shook hands with them, then sat next to Jet. He pointed toward the new girl working behind the bar. "Ain't she a beaut?"

Ronny glanced over. "Yes, she is. Where's she from?"

"She's a yank from Kentucky."

Sully looked over at Jet and nudged him with his elbow. "Sooo?"

Jet's eyes never left the bar. He remained fixated on the girl, tracking her every movement with laser-like focus. Ronny noticed and looked back at the bar, curious to see what had his friend so captivated. He studied the girl, before turning his gaze back to Jet. "It can't be, can it?"

Jet sat silent for another moment, the magnitude of her reappearance bearing down on him like a cruel weight. Finally, he stood. "I need some air." Then he walked outside.

Ronny, understanding Jet's need to flee, silently trailed behind him.

Sully's voice called after them, breaking the tension of the moment. "Jet, golf on Sunday?"

Ronny waved back at him as he ran out the door. "Jet ... hey, wait up."

Jet was pacing in front of his car when Ronny caught up. The more he paced, the angrier he got. "Who the hell does she think she is, showing up here after all this time? What kind of game is she playing at?"

"Hey, calm down. I mean, what are the odds? Seriously!" Jet glared at Ronny. "They say everyone has a twin, right? She could just be someone who kinda looks like her. You're getting upset over nothing." He tried to convince Jet and himself.

Jet leaned against the front of his car. He took a deep breath and covered his face with both hands, then rubbed as if to wake himself. "You're right! You're right." He shook it off, calming himself down.

Worried, Ronny grabbed his shoulder and squeezed it. "Damn, man, after all this time, she still has this effect on you?"

Jet crossed his arms and relaxed against the car, taking a few more deep breaths, when Ronny's phone rang. "It's Penny..."

"Take it, I'm fine."

Ronny nodded. "Hey... Yeah, we went down to the pub for a drink. Good... We'll see you tomorrow, then. Love you too. Bye."

Ronny hung up the phone. "The girls are on their way; they'll be here tomorrow morning sometime."

Jet nodded okay. "Let's go home."

"Hey, what do you want me to tell Sully about Sunday?"

Confused, he asked, "Sunday?"

"Golf ... on Sunday ... with Sully?"

"Oh, yeah. That's fine."

"I'll go tell him."

Jet sat behind the wheel of his car and started the engine as he waited for Ronny. *Would she really come back here after all this time? That would be crazy. She said she was done with this life and wanted to pursue college and find someone stable.*

He let out a heavy sigh, laying his head back on the headrest and closing his eyes. *It's not like she had to run away. All she had to do was ask. I could have given her everything she wanted. It was a shitty way to leave, and she didn't even have the decency to tell me in person. Especially after everything we went through to be together.* The passenger door opened, interrupting his thoughts, and brought him out of his reverie.

Ronny got in. "10 am. Sunday." Jet nodded and drove home.

As they pulled away from the pub, the village quickly disappeared in Jet's rearview mirror. And a mile further out sat a seventeenth-century manor that he had remodeled and added onto around ten years ago. The addition to the property was a home studio and extra living quarters for guests.

He didn't get to stay there much when he and the band were touring, but this last tour was a long one and was finally winding down. With two somewhat local shows left, they had their minds set on taking some much-needed time to rest up and write new music.

Jet pulled into the long drive. The only sound was the soft hum of the engine. He parked the car, and they stepped out into the crisp evening air, the scent of earth and pine mingling together. Without a word between the two, they made their way to their respective rooms.

The following morning, before his wife and Penny arrived, Jet locked himself in the studio. Ronny walked out from the guest house to greet them.

Penny asked, "What are you boys up to this morning? Any plans?"

"Jet's locked himself away in the studio, so it looks like I'm free."

"We were thinking about going into the square to walk the shops and get lunch. Care to join us?"

"Sounds good."

Sitting in the courtyard of an outdoor cafe for lunch, Jet's wife Gabriella, a dark-haired beauty with brown eyes and a shapely figure perfect for rockstar celebrity, excused herself to use the restroom, leaving the two to talk.

"You've been awfully quiet. What's up?"

Ronny looked around to make sure the coast was clear before responding.

"It's Jet."

"What's going on?"

"We went to the pub up the road last night to meet Sully, and he saw someone that upset him."

"Who?"

"Lily."

"What!?"

"Yeah, Sully's got a new barmaid that's stirred up the entire village, so we went to find out what all the fuss was about. I guess she's organizing these activity nights to draw in more people, and it's working. The place was jumping. Anyway, as soon as he saw her, he froze. He's convinced that it's her. I tried to talk him down, but he's holed up in the studio. Which tells me he's really freaked out about it. I'm worried. I haven't seen him like this since she left. His reaction last night was something else. I told him there was no way it was her, but I don't think he believed me. I just don't want to see him spiral down that dark hole again."

"Oh God, what do you wanna do? Do you think it's really her?"

"I'm not sure. I mean, it looks like Lily, but it's been, what … almost twenty years? But don't say anything to Gabby yet until we know for sure. We're playing golf with Sully tomorrow morning; I'll see if I can learn more about her then."

"What if it is her? What does this mean? "

"That's what I'm afraid of. I guess we'll have to cross that bridge when we get to it."

"What about Gabby?"

Sarcastically. "I'm not too worried about her. We both know that marriage is a sham. I would have given it another six months at most, but now?" He shrugged. "She's only in it for his money and what celebrity she can gain from it." Pointing down to the array of shopping bags at their feet. "Hence the shopping spree this morning … and anyway, he only did it to please his mother before she died."

Penny's eyes narrowed, staring at him through his callous remarks. "Oh c'mon, Love, don't tell me you're anything more than a shopping assistant and babysitter to her."

"Well … she does have excellent fashion sense." Penny conceded. "But … I mean, they have to feel something for one another, right?"

"Yeah, of course there's an attraction—she's beautiful. But this is Jet we're talking about," he said, his voice dipping low. "He'll fuck anything willing, no question. We both know what void he's trying to fill or maybe run from. But fall in love … again? Nah, he's never going to love another living soul the way he loves Lily. It's like she's etched onto his DNA, Pen. She's the only one who ever *really* mattered. The rest? They're just … placeholders."

"Yeah. Little twerp broke my heart too," she whispered. Tearing up, she looked up at Ronny through her lashes. He grabbed her hand and held it tight. "She broke all of us, Hun, but him… she shattered completely," Ronny said, his voice heavy with emotion. "He hasn't been the same since. Lily wasn't just his heart—she was his anchor, his compass, the only thing holding him to this planet. Without her, it's like he's been adrift, trying to find pieces of himself in everything and everyone else, but never really able to put himself back together."

Penny nodded then straightened herself, and in a more determined voice she said, "I want to see her."

"Really?"

"Yeah ... I want to see for myself, see if I think it's her too?"

"Okay, I'll talk to Jet."

Gabby returned to the table and sat down. Penny asked, "How do you feel about going to the pub tonight for dinner and a few pints?"

"I'm not a big fan of pubs, so I'll pass. It would be great if there were more higher-quality restaurants in the area to attract a more discerning crowd."

Ronny raised his eyes at Penny as if to say, 'I told you so.' "I guess it's just you and me, Love."

Chapter Three

Shit Happens

(2021)

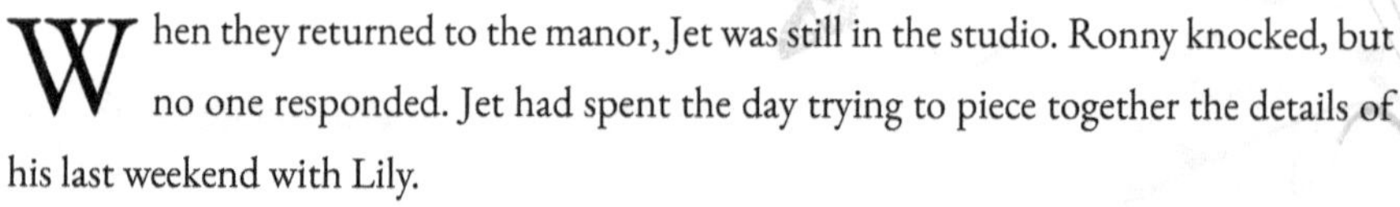

When they returned to the manor, Jet was still in the studio. Ronny knocked, but no one responded. Jet had spent the day trying to piece together the details of his last weekend with Lily.

(2002)

With the summer tour wrapped up and the final promotional interviews behind them, Jet and Lily finally had the garage flat to themselves. The band, now a three-piece, had seen its members move on—Ronny had settled into married life near Penny's parents, and Reggie had returned home to visit with his family. Usually buzzing with bandmates and local fans, the garage had fallen into a rare and blissful silence.

As the door clicked shut behind them, Jet and Lily exchanged a knowing glance, a silent acknowledgment of the tension that had been building for weeks. The air between them seemed to hum with unspoken anticipation. Words felt unnecessary; their connection ran deeper than conversation.

Jet reached for her hand, pulling her gently toward the bed. Their laughter, light and teasing at first, softened as their movements grew more deliberate. They shed their clothes in a quiet rush, a trail of garments marking their path.

Jet's hands traced the familiar curves of Lily's body, his touch reverent yet urgent. His fingers lingered on the spots that made her shiver, drawing soft gasps from her lips. Her skin was warm beneath his palms, her breath hitching as his mouth found her collarbone, then her breast. His tongue teased in slow, deliberate circles, and she arched into him with a quiet moan.

She tugged him closer, her hands exploring the planes of his back, fingers curling against the strength of his shoulders. Jet's lips brushed the hollow of her neck, the faint stubble of his jaw sending sparks through her skin.

The room seemed to shrink around them, the outside world fading into irrelevance. The only sounds were their shared breaths, the rustle of sheets, and the quiet hum of the old ceiling fan above. The distance of their weeks apart dissolved in an instant, replaced by an overwhelming need to feel, to reconnect, to be.

Jet leaned back slightly, his eyes meeting hers, a flicker of mischief dancing in his gaze. His hand brushed along her hip as he reached for the bedside table, pulling out a handful of foil packets, dropping them on the bed beside them. Lily's laughter bubbled up, soft and teasing.

"Prepared, are we?" she quipped, raising an eyebrow.

Jet grinned. "Always," he replied.

He sat back on his knees, tearing open a packet and hurriedly rolling it into place. With a mischievous lift of his brow, he signaled what was coming next. Lily responded, lifting her knees as he hooked his arms under them, drawing her closer as he leaned over her.

The playful moment faded into something deeper as their bodies came together, fitting as if they had been made for this moment, for each other. Lily gasped, her nails pressing lightly into his back, while Jet groaned low in his throat, their movements in perfect rhythm.

Their shared sounds filled the space, intimate and raw, mingling with the soft creak of the bed. Jet shifted, adjusting her gently onto her side, his touch careful but insistent. Lily followed his lead, her body responding instinctively to his every move.

After a few moments, he flipped her onto her knees, intensifying their connection.

As they reached the peak together, the world seemed to fall away, leaving only the two of them intertwined in the afterglow, breathless and sated, but still craving more of each other.

Later, as they lay tangled in the sheets, their breathing slow and heavy, Jet brushed a strand of hair from her damp forehead.

Hours blurred into moments, marked by whispered words and quiet laughter. Between bouts of sleep and soft conversations, they reached for each other again and again, like two halves of a whole rediscovering their balance.

When the quiet growls of their stomachs finally interrupted, Lily sat up with a groan, reaching for the shirt Jet had discarded earlier.

Jet followed, pulling on a pair of joggers. He leaned against the doorway to the kitchen, watching as Lily rummaged through the fridge.

"Think we can make a gourmet meal out of leftovers and whatever's hiding in here?" she asked, glancing over her shoulder with a smirk.

Jet grinned, stepping up behind her and wrapping his arms around her waist. "Challenge accepted."

Lily chuckled, her eyes sparkling with mischief. "I don't know, chef. Let's see what we're working with." They pulled out containers with half-eaten meals, some cheese, and a few random vegetables. Lily held up a slice of cold pizza, raising an eyebrow. "How about pizza à la whatever's-left?"

Jet laughed, grabbing it from her and taking a bite. "Perfect. But only if you add the secret ingredient." He leaned in, brushing his lips against hers in a teasing kiss.

Lily grinned, taking a bite of her own before reaching for a jar of olives. "I got your secret ingredient right here," she teased, popping one into his mouth.

They assembled their impromptu feast, feeding each other bites between laughter and kisses.

There was no rush, no need to be anywhere but here, in this moment. As they sat on the floor, picking at the food they'd pieced together, Lily leaned her head on Jet's shoulder, her fingers tracing idle patterns on his arm. "I missed this," she murmured, her voice soft. "Just us, no schedules, no people. Just you and me."

Jet smiled, brushing a kiss against her hair. "Me too," he replied, his tone low and filled with affection. "Feels like I've been running nonstop. I forgot what it's like to just ... be."

Lily nodded, her fingers still moving in lazy circles on his skin. "Sometimes, I wish we could just disappear for a while, ya know. Go somewhere no one can find us."

Jet chuckled, the sound deep and comforting. "Yeah, Ronny told me about this little cabin in the woods near Somerset. No phones, no internet. Just us, some good music, and a whole lot of nothing to do."

She smiled, tilting her head to look up at him. "That sounds perfect," she whispered, leaning in to press a soft kiss to his lips. "But for now, I'll take this. Wherever you are, I'll take."

Jet returned the kiss, his hand slipping around her waist to pull her closer. They fell into a comfortable silence, the kind that only comes from knowing each other so well.

As Saturday night rolled around, they went to bed early, but in the early morning hours, Lily started screaming, "Get away from us! Leave us alone!" Jet rolled over, grabbing her, trying to ease her thrashing. "Hey. Hey, babe … you're okay. I'm right here." When she finally woke and calmed, he held her tight. Her body shook as she sobbed. This was a bad one. "You're fine, you're fine, I've got you … Shhhh." He kept repeating as he rocked her. She settled herself enough to get a few words out when he asked, "Do you need anything, a drink, maybe? Do you want to tell me about it?"

"No, no, please just—" She shook her head, grabbed him, and buried herself in his arms as deep as she could. "I can't yet." He held her until they both fell back to sleep.

They rolled out of bed Sunday morning to prepare for an afternoon practice but stopped at Jet's parents for brunch first.

She had been acting a little off, and he believed her nightmare from the previous evening was the cause. Although they had decreased in frequency, they would still crop up. This one was particularly disturbing, but she wouldn't give him any real details.

Lily helped Mum in the kitchen while Jet and his dad talked in the parlor. Small talk at first about the band and upcoming studio sessions, but then Pops got more serious. "So, how's our Lily?"

"Pretty good, I guess. Except, last night, she had one of those nightmares and woke up screaming and crying. She kept saying something about 'getting away from us.' I calmed her down enough to go back to sleep, but when I asked her about it this morning, she refused to talk about it. She just said it was over and didn't want to think about it."

"Is she under some kind of stress? You know, now that her classes have ended, and the tour is over. Does she have any plans for Uni?"

"I haven't really asked her. I just assumed she would follow us on our next tour like she did this summer. Our manager said we could add her as a paid consultant, like we do for Penny. I mean, she likes to do our hair and clothing, anyway. She may as well be paid for it."

"Penny is a full-time caterer, though. She has a career aside from the band."

"Yeah, that's true. Do you think maybe she wants to do something else?"

"She's a smart girl, that one. I would hate to see her end up working in a shop till pension when she could be the shop owner."

"Well, she and Mum talk all the time. Has she said anything about university to her?"

"No, not that I'm aware of, but you need to give her the option, son. I think she would be perfectly happy following you around ... until she realized her only identity was tied to being with you. Do you understand?"

"Yeah. you're right. I'll talk to her."

Mum came into the parlor and told them that the food was ready. They walked in to sit down, and Jet could see that Lily had been crying. He walked over to her, hugged her, and kissed her forehead, then whispered, "Hey, are you okay?" She hugged him back and nodded. He assumed she had told Mum about her dream, so he didn't question her further.

That afternoon, as everyone was leaving the garage after the practice, Lily asked, "Hey Jet, could I borrow your car?"

Puzzled, Jet asked, "Why?"

"I need to go to the chemists on the other side of town and I don't want to spend all afternoon on the bus."

"Are you okay?"

"Yes, it's just that that's the only store that carries what I need."

"How about I drive you over? I wanted to talk to you about something anyway."

"Umm, okay ... I guess."

They headed out, and on the way, Jet tried to talk to her.

"Hey, Lil?"

She was looking out the window, either concentrating or lost in thought.

"Lily?"

"Hmm?"

"Hey, so that tour was something else, wasn't it?"

"Mmm hmm."

"So now that we're back, have you thought about what you want to do now that classes are over?"

"Em, no, not yet; I think we turn here ..."

She seemed very distracted and not really listening, so he figured he would table the conversation until he could have her undivided attention.

When they arrived, they had to park in a car park away from the store and walk. On their way in, Jet ran into an old schoolmate. Lily had never met this person before, so she excused herself and told him to stay with his friend and that she would get what she needed and meet him back there.

Jet finished his conversation a few minutes later when he saw his uncle quickly walking through the square. "Hey ... Uncle Andrei?"

The man stopped. "John? So good to see you. What are you doing on this side of town?"

"My girlfriend just ran into the store to grab something ... Hey, I thought you weren't coming until next week. Does my mum know you're here?"

"No, no, I am here on layover from business trip. I will return next week to visit. I must hurry now. We are going back to airport. I will see you then?"

"Yeah ... sure ... see you then."

His uncle gave him a big smile and a two-handed pistol shot with his fingers as he hurried away and yelled, "My big rockstar nephew!"

Jet kinda laughed and headed into the store to find Lily. He walked the aisles for several minutes but couldn't find her. He got frustrated, thinking they were possibly missing each other the more he wandered, so he stood at the front entrance and waited.

Another five minutes went by, and now he was frustrated and concerned. He walked around one more time and then went outside and looked around the square to see if she was looking for him. Nothing. He couldn't find her anywhere. He called Ronny and told him what had happened. Within an hour, the band and their friends formed a makeshift search party.

They had no luck after another hour of searching, so Jet called his parents and 999. The police took the initial report and continued to search the square and stores for any sign of her, but to no avail. They said they would continue the search if she didn't show up by morning. However, they weren't concerned as most girls usually turned up at a friend's house after having an argument with their boyfriends.

Jet kept assuring them that no argument had taken place. But they told him to go home and call her friends, anyway. Ronny and Penny took Jet to the garage and stayed with him that night.

Jet stormed through the room, tearing through drawers and tossing aside clothes in a frenzy. "Where are you, Lily? Damn it!" His voice cracked with desperation as he overturned a chair, sending it crashing to the floor.

He paused for a moment, chest heaving, eyes scanning the room for any sign of her. "This can't be happening…" He muttered to himself, his hands trembling as he ran them through his hair.

Finally, he sank onto the bed, clutching her pillow to his chest. The familiar scent of her perfume hit him, and he buried his face into it, his breath hitching as tears seeped into the fabric.

"Why wasn't I there?" he whispered, the words choked with guilt. "I promised you, Lily … I promised I'd always protect you."

He clenched his fists, the pillow now soaked with his tears. "Where are you? Just… just let me find you, please. I can't lose you like this."

His voice broke as he stared at the ceiling, his mind racing with fear and regret. "If something's happened to you … I'll never forgive myself. I should've been there. I should've known …"

The silence of the room echoed back at him, offering no comfort, no answers. He closed his eyes, a single thought repeating in his mind. "Please, Lily … be safe. Please come back to me."

Something was off with her that day, but he had attributed it to the dream. Now, he was second-guessing himself for not pushing her to talk to him earlier.

Ronny and Penny called everyone they knew looking for her and tried to reassure him they would not give up the search.

Jet's parents informed Lily's grandfather of the situation and assisted the family in searching her belongings for potential clues. Mum found a diary under Lily's mattress with only a few passages.

In those passages, Lily spoke about her confusion regarding her and Jet's relationship and the need for time to figure things out. She also expressed an interest in returning to the US to attend college.

<u>April 14th,</u>

I've been feeling so lost lately. Jet and I have this connection, this love, but sometimes I wonder if it's enough. We keep fighting, and I can't shake this feeling that maybe we're too different, or maybe I'm just too young to know what I really want. I love him; I do. But is that enough to make this work? I need time to figure things out, but I'm scared of what I might discover.

<u>May 2nd,</u>

I've been thinking more and more about the future, and it's becoming clear that I need to make some decisions for myself. Jet's world is so intense, so overwhelming, and I feel like I'm losing myself in it. Maybe going back to the US for college would help me find some clarity, some independence. I've always wanted to go to school there, and maybe this is my chance to focus on me for a while. But what does that mean for Jet and me? I don't know. I just need space to breathe.

<u>May 21st,</u>

It feels like everything is coming to a head. I can't keep avoiding the truth—I'm not sure if Jet and I are meant to be together, at least not right now. Maybe this time apart will give me the answers I need. Going to college in the US could be a fresh start, a way to figure out who I am without being defined by this relationship. But the thought of leaving him behind. It hurts more than I can put into words. I just don't know what to do.

<u>June 5th,</u>

Today, I met someone different. He's stable, grounded, and honestly, it was refreshing. There was no drama, no intensity—just a simple conversation. It made me realize how chaotic things have been with Jet lately. I'm not saying I want to be with this guy, but it made me think about what life could be like with someone who doesn't always make my heart race for the wrong reasons. Maybe that's what I need—a sense of stability, someone who won't leave me feeling so torn all the time. But then, is that really what I want? Or is this just a reaction to all the uncertainty? I'm so confused.

"This doesn't make sense," her grandfather said. "She would never go back there. How could this be? All of her things are still here!" He was confused and worried and said, "Even so, she would never just leave her family without saying something." He couldn't believe what he was reading.

Mum called the garage and informed them of what they had found. Jet couldn't believe it either. He wouldn't believe it; he knew her better than anyone. This was not like her at all. Something had to have happened.

The next day, they contacted the police, and the search was called off. The police had done some preliminary online searches overnight and found a ticket in her name that was used for a flight to Atlanta, near where her stepfather and mother lived. At this point, knowing her fear and hatred for her stepfather, Jet undoubtedly questioned their presumptions.

(2021)

Jet woke up on the studio couch in the middle of the night, surrounded by an assortment of empty and half-empty liquor bottles. He found his way to the main house and then his room, where Gabby was sleeping. He had forgotten she was coming and didn't want to deal with her.

He returned to the studio and accidentally woke Ronny while entering. "Hey, you finally came out of the studio."

"Yeah ... I'm going back in."

"Can I come in?"

"Whatever." He opened the door, and they both entered.

Ronny started the conversation by saying, "So ... Penny and I went to the pub tonight."

"Yeah? Soo?"

"Penny took one look at that new girl and thought it was her too, but that's not the only thing. While we were there, Pen got a call from Catherine. She also thinks it may be her."

"What do you mean?"

"Lily. You may be right. It may be her."

"Wait, what? You were so sure I was wrong."

"Well, it seems Lily was, actually, in Leeds a few months ago."

"What?"

"Yeah, she was buying groceries for her aunt and ran into Catherine. They spoke briefly, and she told her she had been gone a long time but was back."

"Wait, what are you saying?"

"I'm saying that we need to talk to Sully tomorrow to see what he knows."

Jet looked hard at him. "What time do we have to be there?"

"Ten."

Jet fell back onto the couch. "Wake me at eight."

"Yep." Ronny left and went back to his room.

Jet lay there, his mind still consumed by thoughts of Lily, head not yet pounding. He popped a couple of pain relievers and downed a water bottle, hoping they would prevent the inevitable hangover he knew was coming. As he settled back, more memories flooded his mind, each one a painful reminder of what he had lost.

Chapter Four

Faded Echoes

(2003)

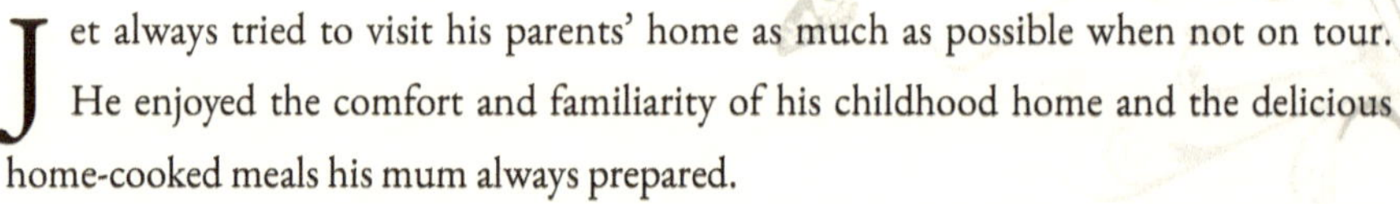

Jet always tried to visit his parents' home as much as possible when not on tour. He enjoyed the comfort and familiarity of his childhood home and the delicious home-cooked meals his mum always prepared.

On this particular day, he had nothing planned for the evening as his flatmate and drummer for the band Reggie was away. Eagerly, Jet made his way to his mum's, hoping for another wonderful meal. As he walked in the door, he saw Pops sitting in the parlor watching the telly.

"Where's mum?" he said as he walked by, the smell of stew wafting throughout the house.

"In the kitchen, I believe, son," Pops answered without looking away from the screen.

Jet nodded on his way to see her.

"Hey, Love. Are you staying for dinner? It's almost ready." Mum asked. Jet kissed her on the cheek, then grabbed a drink from the fridge and sat at the table.

"You know I never say no to your cooking." He smiled, knowing it would make her happy. Making conversation, he added, "You guys are eating early today; you headed out for the evening?"

Mum paused what she was doing and carefully chose her words. "We're going to go play cards with some friends tonight."

He looked at her suspiciously. "Don't you usually play cards with Minnie and Abe?"

"Well, yes... that's where we're going ... I just—"

"Mum, you don't have to hide where you're going on my account. I'm fine. I know they're your friends."

"I know. I just didn't know how you would feel about it."

He sat silent for a moment, then asked, "Any word from Lily?" He tried to be nonchalant.

"Uh, yeah, actually. Minnie said she got a letter the other day. Evidently, she has started school and is taking business classes."

"Huh, well, good for her. She was always good at that kind of stuff."

"Hun, are you okay? Talking about this, I mean?"

"Yeah, I mean, she's gone ... she made her decision. Nothing I can do about it but wish her well, right?"

"That's a very enlightened attitude. I hope you mean it."

"I don't have any other options, do I? She took those with her."

"Awe, Hun."

Jet hesitated before pulling the worn and wrinkled envelope from his pocket. "I've been carrying it around for a while," he admitted, his voice low. He turned the envelope over in his hands, the corners soft from being handled so much. Finally, he placed it on the table, his fingers lingering just a second longer than necessary before sliding it toward her.

"What's this?" she asked.

"Closure. I hope. There's no address on it. But since you're going to see them tonight ... I thought maybe Minnie could send it to Lily for me, since no one will tell me where she is."

"I'll see that Minnie gets it."

"Thanks." Jet got up and went to sit with Pops until dinner was ready.

Mum watched him leave the room, her heart aching at the weight her son carried. She glanced at the letter on the table. Picking it up, she put it in her purse by the door.

Later, after they ate and Jet left, Mum took the letter out of her purse, tucked it into the pocket of her apron and went upstairs to get ready. In the quiet of the bathroom, she hesitated before opening it. Jet's handwriting was bold and unsteady, his emotions practically leaping off the page.

Dear Lily,

I hope you are doing well. Actually, I'm sorry, I don't hope all is well. What I really hope is that you will come to your senses and come home. I miss you, and I don't understand why you couldn't tell me you were unhappy. Everyone here is wondering the same thing. Especially your grandfather. He is sick without you. I don't understand how you could just leave everyone and everything behind without so much as a goodbye or how you could just leave me without some kind of explanation; it's just crazy. It's not like you to behave like this. If you wanted school, a career and a stable man, I would have been more than willing to give you that. You didn't have to run away to find it.

I still have a hard time believing you did. I feel like this whole thing is some kind of lie or trick or dream, but for the life of me, I can't figure out why. Every day, I half expect that you'll just walk in the door like you never left, and everything will just go back to the way it was.

Lily, I know we were happy. I don't care what anyone else says. They weren't there during our private times together. When we made love or had our private conversations. They'll never convince me you weren't happy. So, you need to. I need to hear it from you, Lily. Call me, please, reverse the charges if you have to, and convince me you're better off there without me. I need you to tell me it's over; otherwise, it will never be over for me. I love you, and I know you love me. If you tell me. If I hear it from you, I'll set aside my feelings and wish you the very best. That's always been my wish for you, anyway.

Please, Lily, call me. +44-113-812 1965

Yours Forever,

Jet

Mum stared at the letter in her hands, the words blurring as her chest tightened. She folded the letter carefully, smoothing the creases as though that would ease the turmoil written across its surface. "Oh, John," she whispered, her voice trembling as her fingers lingered on the envelope before slipping it back into her pocket. With a deep breath, she stood straight and made sure she was alone before entering her bedroom and placing it into the bottom drawer of her armoire.

Chapter Five

Fixated

(2021)

Eight o'clock came early, as the sun gleamed through the floor-to-ceiling windows, Jet jolted awake when Ronny's insistent knocking echoed through the studio. "Yeah! Yeah … I'm up!" He bellowed, rubbing the sleep from his eyes. Groggily, he made his way to the shower, the warm water washing away the remnants of his restless night.

After dressing in a haze, he trudged towards the main house. As he entered the kitchen, the aroma of freshly brewed coffee enveloped him, mingling with the sound of hushed conversation. Everyone was standing around the breakfast bar when he walked in.

Gabriela spoke first, "You look like hell."

"Rough night," he explained.

"Didn't realize writing was so rough," she snarked.

He closed his eyes as he took a deep breath, then opened them to say as calmly as he could, "Please, don't start."

"I'm not starting anything. You couldn't even come out of your studio to say hello, much less—"

He walked out of the room, ignoring her tirade. As he passed Ronny, he said, "Meet me in the car. I'm going to grab my clubs."

Ronny looked at Penny with raised eyebrows. "Here we go." He kissed her on the cheek as he left.

"Good luck," she whispered.

Jet started to feel better on the golf course once he was out in the cool, fresh morning air. Ronny teed up first while Sully and Jet stood back and watched. "Sorry, we didn't get a chance to talk the other night. I was a bit out of sorts."

"Oh, no worries, lad."

"So, business looks good."

"Aah, Laddie, if it keeps up like des, I'll be able to retire."

"Really? You retire? I figured you'd die in that pub. We'd come in to see your body propped up on one of those stools in the corner so you could watch over your baby."

"Aye, six months ago, I would've agreed wet you, but dhat new girl o' mine has a hell of a head fer business. It's like she can read what de people want, and den make it happen. At lettle to no cahst to boot!"

"Huh ... who is she? Where did she come from?"

Sully gave him a giant grin. "Yooehr married son." Then slapped him on his back. "Hands ahff, she's all mine."

"I bet Fiona has something to say about that."

"Nay, she loves de lass." As he walked up to tee off.

Under his breath, Jet agreed. "What's not to love?"

Ronny tried his luck at the next hole while Jet was up. "So, Penny and I came in last night. I think the entire village was there! Didn't see you though."

"Fiona an me 'ad a date night."

Ronny gave him a crazed look. "Date night?"

"Dat's what Daria calls it, anyway. She said I needed to spend some quality time wet me, Wifey."

"Ha! Yeah, I suppose it's always a good idea to spend some quality time with our wives."

"I can't tell you de last time me and Fi had a night on de town. She wahre me out!"

Ronny laughed and slapped him on the back. "Good on ya, ole man!" Sully rolled his eyes as he took his turn.

Ronny nodded at Jet to join him. "Well, son, our question is answered."

"So, it is her."

Ronny nodded, rolling back on his heels. "Mmm hmmm."

Watching Sully, he whispered, "Well, fuck! I don't need this right now."

Jet was up. They finished their round and headed home.

Jet spent the better part of the next week in the studio with Ronny. Jet's head was not in the game, so Reggie came in midweek to help lay down some tracks. Ronny filled him in on the situation.

Reggie always had a little bit of a crush on Lily, so when he heard the story, he was like... "Nooo, shit! After all this time? Have you talked to her yet?"

Jet shook his head.

"Are ya gonna talk to her? Or ya just gonna pine over her again?"

"Fuck off, I'm not pining!" Jet looked at Ronny for backup but didn't receive it.

Ronny grimaced and shrugged his shoulders. "You're kinda pining."

"Fuck both of you off!" They laughed at him as he put his headphones back on to ignore them.

Despite the quaint charm of the village, Gabriela often found herself longing for the hustle and bustle of city life and took off to see her family in London. Left alone, Jet spent most of his evenings at the pub, watching and sitting with Sully at his secluded corner table.

During one of their many conversations, Jet offered to buy the pub from Sully. "Why would ye want des old place?"

"Well, it's close to home, for one thing, and it looks like it might be an excellent investment, plus, you've been talking about retirement. Sully, this is a second home for a lot of folks around here. Where would we all go if you were to close? Besides, this way, you'll have a local pub to visit in your old age and some extra change in your pocket."

Sully pondered the question as a ruckus started up near the bar. Two locals were getting into a shoving match after knocking over a table and spilling glasses onto the floor. Before it could get any worse, Daria grabbed a bat from under the counter and headed towards the men from behind the bar. She launched herself onto the bar top and slid off the other side. When she got to them, she slammed the bat on the table behind them, making a loud crashing noise.

A hush fell over the room as Jet's reflexes kicked in, ready to shield her from any potential threat, but Sully grabbed his arm and pulled him back down. They watched as she spun the bat around, rolled her shoulders, and got ready to swing, then calmly, cocking her head, said, "Who's first?"

Both men stopped, wide-eyed, and backed away from each other, putting their hands up in surrender. Then they both apologized. "Sorry, Daria."

"Yeah, sorry, Love."

She pointed at the floor with the bat and said, "That's what I thought. Clean this mess up, then meet me at the bar—Now!"

She walked back to the bar, twirling the bat as the crowd cheered and helped the employees pick the tables up. Once she got back behind the bar, she watched and waited for the men to meet her there. When they stepped up, she put two pints in front of them and made them shake hands. They did one better and hugged each other. The crowd cheered again!

Sully turned back to Jet as if nothing had happened and said, "Now, where were we? Ahh yeah, what would ye be knowin' about runnin' a pub?"

Jet pointed at Daria. "Looks like that part's covered. She doesn't seem to need any help."

Sully leaned back in his chair and thought for a moment. "Let me run des by Fi, and I'll get back to ya."

"If you would do me a favor and not say anything to the employees yet. I'd like to introduce myself individually if you decide to take the offer."

"Sure din." Sully patted the table and then got up to greet the other guests.

After negotiating with Sully over the next few weeks, he and Fi agreed to the sale. He kept his word about not telling the employees until the sale was final.

When Jet took ownership, he told Sully it was okay to inform the employees, but he would like to meet with Daria first. His reasoning behind this decision was to catch her off guard and elicit a genuine reaction.

Jet had been fixated on her since that first night. The memory of her haunted him, constantly pulling at him with a mixture of longing and uncertainty. All he could think of was whether the mark he had left on her was still there, buried deep in her thoughts, or if she had moved on entirely, with her own hidden motives now at play.

As the weight of his newfound control over the situation settled into him, a sudden surge of empowerment coursed through him. For the first time in a long while, it was *his* move. He was the one holding the cards now, and it felt almost ... intoxicating.

But that sense of power was quickly overshadowed by the storm of conflicting emotions raging inside him. What was this obsession? Was his fixation on her born from resentment—years of unanswered questions, pain, and confusion—or was it something deeper, a lingering flame of affection that refused to die?

As he sat there, grappling with his own thoughts, deep down, he knew he already had his answer.

Chapter Six

Sold

(2021)

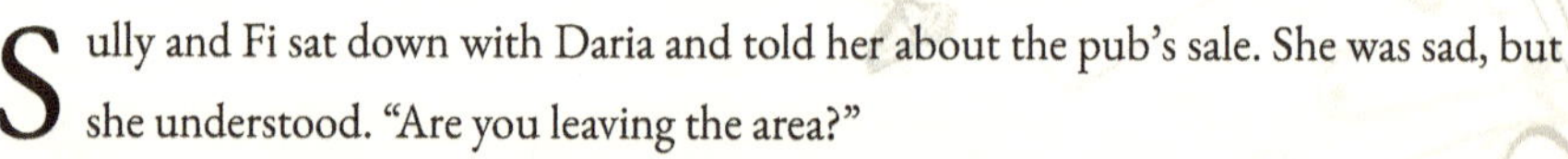

S ully and Fi sat down with Daria and told her about the pub's sale. She was sad, but she understood. "Are you leaving the area?"

"Oh no, dear. We're not going anywhere," Fi said.

"We'll be right here if you need us," Sully confirmed.

"Good, because I don't think I could stand losing any more people right now." Fi gave Sully a worried look, then put her hand on Daria's knee. "No Love, I'll be expecting my Wednesday afternoon social hour in the back room as usual."

Daria smiled and held her hand. "So, nothing is changing except for who's paying the bills then."

"That's right, lass. The new owner will be a silent owner, as in, he'll not be involved in de day-to-day running of de pub. That'll be your job now, and if you still want to stay in de office, it too is yours."

Daria nodded. "So, when do we meet our new boss?"

"Next week. De pub will close for a few days because he wants to upgrade the electric box and add some security, but after dat, he will meet with everyone individually. You will be de first to meet with him on Monday."

"You mean like an interview?"

"No, lass, not in your case. He's been here over the last few weeks and seen your work, and he's impressed. The lad just wants a meet and greet, dhat's all. He's an old friend. We play golf together when he's in town. He travels a lot for work."

"Okay, do I need to get a room somewhere while the upgrades take place?"

Fi spoke up and said, "No, dear, you can stay with us until he's finished if you like."

Daria took advantage of the days off. She spent a couple of days in Leeds with her aunt, then returned and hung out with Sully and Fi.

After completing the upgrades, she reentered the pub, stepping into a freshly decorated office slash bedroom space. The transformation into an efficiency had her pleasantly taken aback. It was complete with a small fridge and counter space, a desk area for pub business, a comfortable sitting chair with a lamp, a television, and a proper bed. The walls featured a soothing pale pastel lilac paint complemented by white wood shutters adorned with delicate white sheers. "How did he know I loved this color?" And her favorite fresh flowers, lilacs, of course, arranged on the desk.

She walked around the pub and checked out the new equipment. It looked like they could use the new electric panel to accommodate larger bands. And with the new lighting and sound equipment, she thought to herself. *Oh my God, we could make a killing here. We could also clear the back area of the pub, put up a pergola, make a beer garden for sunny days, and maybe even rent it out for special occasions. I can't wait to share some new ideas with this guy on Monday.* Eager to reopen, she got to work.

It was Saturday, and as expected, the regular crowd showed up to check out the new upgrades. They were a lively group, more so than usual. Some brought their own instruments to test out the stage and sound equipment, which essentially turned into an impromptu open mic night.

At the end of the evening, Daria rang the bell for last drinks and closed the pub. She locked up after everyone left. Then she headed to her room.

Daria took a shower, and when she got out, she wrapped up in a big fluffy towel and headed back into the bar area. She made herself a drink, brought the bottle with her and grabbed her cell phone, then sat at one of the booths with her feet propped up on the seat sideways.

Her cell phone rang. It was Jack. "Hi, Baby! How are you? Renee, what? Oh, that sounds like so much fun! Well, she was always good at barrel racing. Did she win any medals? Well, you tell her I said better luck next time." She spoke to him for another twenty minutes.

She missed Jack and Renee dearly, and when she hung up, she sat scrolling through the new pictures they sent her. She paused on an old picture of Jet. Daria stared at it, laying it on the table and finishing her drink. She poured another, and after a few more pours, she became nostalgic and began tracing her finger over the picture and humming her song.

Unbeknownst to her, the new electric and band setup were not the only upgraded systems. There were cameras, too. Hidden in the ceiling and all around the perimeter of the building outside. There was a monitoring closet that she had not thought to look in yet. And being the new owner, Jet had the same setup at his compound and was already monitoring the system.

He tuned in just as she was finishing a conversation with someone and watched as she scrolled through pictures. She became emotional when she stopped on his picture. He heard her say through her tears. "I'm sorry, babe, I just don't have it in me ... no matter what I do, I can't let you go." She picked up the phone to speak to him face-to-face. "I'm glad you stuck with the band, though. It looks like things worked out for ya'll ... I'm happy for you. I hope you're happy, too." She clicked the phone off, swallowed the last bit of her drink, and slid out of the booth.

Chapter Seven

Can't Stay Angry
(2021)

J et tried his best to stay angry with her; it was safe, a barrier that protected his heart. But the more he saw her, the more those old feelings tugged at him. Her laughter, soft and genuine as she finished her conversation, echoed in his ears—he always loved hearing her laugh. Even as a child, her little giggles would melt his heart. But this, actually hearing it again, cut through him like a knife. *Damn you,* he cursed silently, a mix of love and anger twisting inside him. *How dare you laugh like that, like nothing's changed? How dare you act like you didn't rip my fucking heart out?*

Watching her scroll through her phone, he couldn't stop the flood of emotions that surged within him. *Why are you here?* He thought, eyes fixed on the screen. *Is it because of me? Or are you just passing through, thinking I wouldn't notice?* The questions swirled in his mind.

Look at you, twenty years and you haven't changed, Lil, he mused, unable to tear his gaze away from her. *But I've changed. Or maybe you haven't—maybe that's your problem, dumb-ass. Still hung up on a girl who walked out on you without a word.*

And now, glaring through the screen, struggling to reconcile the woman in front of him with the one who had left him shattered. *How could you just leave like that?* His thoughts were sharp, cutting through the haze of his emotions. *We were good. Weren't we? I know we were. What happened, Lily?* He tapped his fingers on the mouse pad. *Did I miss something? Was I so caught up in my own world that I didn't see you slipping away?*

Guilt washed over him, as always. *Maybe it was my fault. Maybe I wasn't there enough, or maybe I was there too much. Maybe if I had just ... ugh!* he shook his head, trying to dispel the thoughts that had haunted him for years. *Just stop ... Jesus ... Not again ... Not now.*

The internal battle raged on, his heart refusing to let go even as his mind urged him to. *Let her go,* he told himself for the thousandth time, but the words held no power. *You can't keep holding on to something that's not yours. She's gone.*

But even as he thought it, he knew he didn't believe it. *No,* he admitted to himself. *She's not gone. She's here, right in front of me. And maybe, just maybe, there's still a chance ...*

He closed his eyes, trying to shut out the hope that threatened to overwhelm him. But the memories were too powerful to ignore. *Don't be an idiot, Jet. She left once; she'll leave again. And this time, you might not survive it.* His mind raced, trying to make sense of it all.

He pressed his fingertips to the screen, tracing the outline of her face, remembering a time when loving her was the only thing that felt right, even when it felt wrong. *I loved you; ya know. More than I ever loved anyone. I still do ... even though I don't want to. Even though I shouldn't.* His chest tightened, the pain of her absence still as fresh as the day she left. *Why didn't you fight for us, Lil? You chased me, remember? For so long ... and when you finally caught me ... when we caught each other... I just don't get it.*

Jet sighed, feeling the weight of the years without her pushing down on him. Sully mentioned he thought she might be running from something or someone. Was it him? But he watched her over the past several weeks. She seemed happy and content with her job at the pub. Which was it? He was torn. *Did you really move on?* A bitter taste sat in his mouth. *Are you really happier without me? And, if that's true, then why are you here?*

But just then, as he watched her trace his picture through the screen and heard her words, confusion flooded his mind. "I'm sorry, babe, I just don't have it in me ... no matter what I do, I can't let you go." Did he hear her right? *What?* Speechless, his mind went blank, and his heart leapt. Was this the flicker of hope that he sought? The pub's dim lighting flickered across her face as she continued to speak.

Jet reached out again, touching her image, wanting to crawl through the monitor and hold her. He even thought of driving over, but no, he pulled back. *Stop it!* That would ruin the plan. *Stick to the plan, dammit!* If he showed his hand now, it would put the power back in her hands. And he wasn't ready to give it back just yet. Or was it just a fool's dream ... thinking he had any power to begin with?

His heart ached with a mix of nostalgia and longing as memories flooded back—their shared laughter, the way she used to trace circles on his palm when she was nervous, and the quiet moments when words weren't necessary. His mind drifted even further, to those early years when he longed to be near her, but didn't yet understand the depth of his feelings or the powerful sense of protection he felt. At the time, he had attributed it to her fears and past trauma.

But later, when they finally came together, everything changed. The countless nights he held her after her nightmares and the first time they made love solidified a bond that felt almost transcendent. The intimacy they shared was unlike anything he had ever known—before or after.

She was his home, making him feel whole and complete. He smiled, remembering his father joking about how they acted like an old married couple. But it was true—they had been close for almost twelve years, at that point, longer than most marriages. And now, every thought, every memory, every familiar scent—felt like fragments of a different lifetime.

He missed the joy of Sunday morning brunches with his family, the sweet aroma of back bacon and freshly brewed coffee for the American girl filling the house and everyone gathering around, sharing stories and catching up on the week's events. And the homelike ease of Wednesday nights. Dinner and cards with Lily's family. Her aunt and she always prepared a delicious meal, and everyone sat around the table, chatting and laughing. He missed the love that filled the room, and he felt truly blessed to have been a part of it. These memories were precious to him, and he held them close to his heart. They were a reminder of a simpler time when life was less complicated and the people he loved were always by his side.

But all of that vanished when she disappeared. His world crashed. Her absence left him depressed and detached. Without her support, her confidence in him, pushing him to never give up and her role as his biggest cheerleader, a part of him felt missing, or worse, as if it had died. Nothing could replace that—not even his music.

It was crazy. Jet hung on to the guilt of letting her go into the store by herself like a lifeline. The pain and loneliness of being without her, although in and of itself, was unbearable. It was something. The ache in his chest, the tears that pricked, the doubt that he carried—about himself and his life choices. It was at least a tangible sign he could still feel—anything.

To this day, deep down, he still believes the entire thing was a sham. Dammit, he knew her; he couldn't fathom her just walking away like that. But then the letters started coming. Lily never wrote to him directly, but he heard stories secondhand from her grandfather and Mum that caused him to question his own beliefs over the years.

Finding himself caught in a slow, destructive cycle of alcohol and drugs, he turned to anything that could numb the pain or help him forget her, even if only for a fleeting moment.

After a couple of near-overdoses, Ronny and Reggie, with the support of their record label, managed to get him into rehab. Since then, he's been doing well. Though there have been a few setbacks with alcohol, he's stayed away from drugs and, for the most part, has remained on the straight and narrow. But with news of Lily's return and his recent studio binge, Ronny and Reggie have been keeping a close eye on him, ready to step in if he falters.

Chapter Eight

Lost in Central Park

(2006)

As their bus eased to a stop in front of the hotel, the neon glow of the city reflected off its sleek exterior. Exhausted, yet with adrenaline still buzzing through them from their mind-blowing performance at Terminal 5 in New York City, the members of Fractured Butterfly meandered off their charter one by one.

Amidst the distant honking of taxis and the promise of the next day off, the anticipation of a full day of sightseeing hung in the air. Jet lingered. Ronny and Reggie hung back to wait for him. The last to disembark, Jet stopped and stood with his two mates, watching as their crew unloaded more bags. Jet slung his pack over his shoulder and lit a cigarette.

"You going up?" Reggie asked.

Jet looked around, noticing the vibrant pulse of the city that never slept, then handed Ronny his bag. "No, I'm gonna finish this and maybe take a walk before I come up."

"Okay," they both said and headed into the hotel.

"See ya in a bit?" Ronny urged, more of a comment than a question, letting Jet know he was probably going to be waiting up for him.

"Yeah, yeah ... I'll be up soon." Jet encouraged, knowing that Ronny was always the worrier of the group.

He wandered down the street until he stumbled upon a cozy bar with an empty window seat. He made his way in and took a seat and after he ordered a beer; he fished a cigarette from his pocket. As he reached in, his fingers brushed against a few pills and a tiny bag of powder. *A party night it is, then,* he thought to himself, a wry smirk playing on his lips.

His beer came, and he ordered a shot to go with it. When the waitress returned with his order, he popped the pills, downed the shot, and sat sipping his beer.

He watched as the people walked by, the bustle of the city swirling past him, and saw Lily's face on every brown-haired girl. Confronting himself, a pang of longing mingled with frustration and regret surged through him. *This can't be your life now, sitting here watching other people live. You'd think you'd be happy with the guys and the band's success. You have everything ... well, almost everything, but you're just ... empty.* Then, claiming that grief. *I'm ... empty.* Jet breathed a long sigh, sat there for a few more numbing beers, and hit the bathroom before leaving.

He remembered the powder. He had no idea what it was; it could have been cocaine, heroin, or even baking soda. He didn't care at that point. Whatever pills he had taken had already kicked in with the alcohol, and he was already feeling no pain. The room spun around him, colors blurring into a dizzying kaleidoscope as he surrendered to the numbing haze enveloping his senses.

He wanted to prolong his jaunt through the vacuum of painless vacuity he imagined he could find in the myriad of pharmaceuticals left as gifts from fans and backstage groupies. With each pill taken, every drink swallowed, or every powder snorted, he could eventually feel the weight of reality lift, replaced by a fleeting sense of euphoria that he would chase relentlessly.

Lips numb and head spinning, he stumbled into a stall, collapsing onto the toilet seat. With trembling hands, he reached into the little baggy, scooping out a small pile of powder and pressing it to his nose.

He inhaled sharply, feeling the burn as the substance rushed into his system. Without hesitation, he repeated the action on the other side, finishing off what remained in the bag. Rubbing the residue along his gums, he leaned back, his pulse racing as he waited to be consumed by the void.

A few minutes or an hour later, he sat upright, left the bar, and walked towards Central Park, craving the solace of the night air. It was late, or maybe early, and the park was quiet ... so quiet and empty. He wandered around for what felt like hours, but probably not.

He strayed from the path and soon found himself lost amidst a thicket of trees. His gait grew unsteady, stumbling from trunk to trunk until he finally found one to cling to for stability. But his legs could no longer hold his frame, and he collapsed to the ground, finally yielding at last to the embrace of oblivion...

Two days later, Jet woke to the harsh glare of bright lights, buzzers and bleeps from hospital equipment. Ronny and Reggie were in the two chairs next to his bed.

Ronny was asleep, and Reggie was reading a magazine. He looked up to see Jet's eyes open. "Hey, Dude … What the fuck! You scared the shit out of us."

Ronny woke and spoke more diplomatically, giving Reggie a stern side-eye. "Hey, how are you feeling?"

Jet tried to speak, but it came out as a whisper. "Sore." He grabbed his throat. "Where am I?"

"A runner found you next to death in North Central Park about twenty feet off the trail, passed out. You almost died, Jet. If that guy hadn't found you when he did … you would have," Ronny said.

"Thank God he's a fan and recognized you," Reggie barked, his tone a mix of frustration and relief. "He said he normally just lets the drunks sleep it off when he runs that early, but he had been at the show the night before and remembered your outfit. That's what made him stop. He called for an ambulance—Dammit, Jet, what were you thinking? Is this shit still about Lily?"

Jet closed his eyes. "Don't. Go there. I wasn't thinking … or rather, I was trying to stop thinking." Tears ran down the side of his face as his eyes opened, and he stared at the ceiling.

Ronny grabbed Jet's arm, giving him a reassuring squeeze. "Get some rest. The tour is over, my friend. When they release you, you're being checked into a rehab facility."

"What!" He glared at them. "No! I'm not going to no damn rehab."

"You don't really have a choice. It's in the contract. You're going if you don't want to get sued by the record label. They control your healthcare and are your medical surrogate when on tour—you signed it—they acted on your behalf. It was either that or jail," Ronny said.

"Jail?"

"Yeah—jail Jet! You had narcotics in your system, opioids to be exact, and they found you in a public place."

"They should've left me there," Jet said, almost under his breath, his voice tinged with anguish, and his gaze fixed on the sterile ceiling tiles above.

Ronny and Reggie exchanged a worried glance, their brows furrowing in concern as they processed Jet's words.

A week later, Jet was ready to leave the hospital. Ronny and Reggie were there to pick him up. "Hey guys, I just wanted to apologize for getting the tour canceled. I know everyone worked really hard on it and I fucked it up."

"No worries, mate." Reggie grabbed his shoulder and gave him a bit of a shake. "I was ready for a break anyway. Plus, it's probably the most rock 'n roll thing you've ever done." He half laughed.

Ronny laughed through his nose. "Yeah, don't sweat it, mate. Things will be okay. And believe it or not, according to the label, the publicity is actually boosting record sales."

"Well, I appreciate you saying that." He sighed and handed Ronny a pamphlet. "I guess I'm off to Pompano Beach. At least I'll have a view." Jet spent the next thirty days at a facility in Florida and the next six months in therapy.

Chapter Nine

The Beast

(2021)

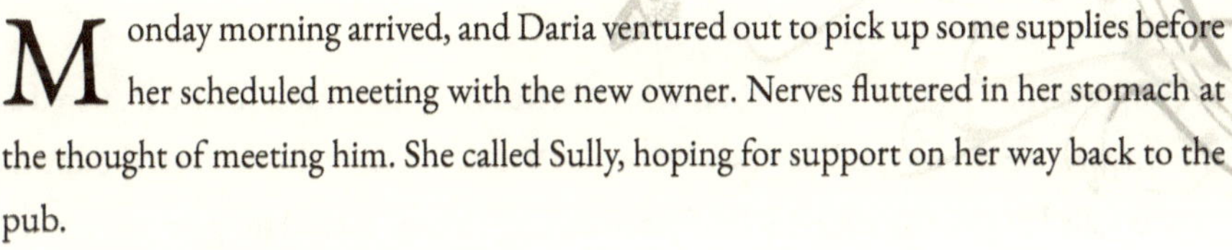

Monday morning arrived, and Daria ventured out to pick up some supplies before her scheduled meeting with the new owner. Nerves fluttered in her stomach at the thought of meeting him. She called Sully, hoping for support on her way back to the pub.

"Hello, lass, where ye be?"

"I'm on my way. Should be there in about five minutes."

"Well, I'll just be warnin' ya that Rory's in the car park waitin' for ya."

"Seriously, today?"

"Aye, it looks like he's lookin' to play."

"Well, shit. Is the new owner there yet?"

"Aye."

"What do you want me to do, Sully? Does he have time for me to give Rory a run for his money?"

Jet was standing next to Sully when the call came in and could hear the conversation. Sully covered the receiver, looked at Jet, and asked, "Well, son, de ye have time for de lass to be a few minutes late?"

Jet nodded, then whispered. "Rory? What do you mean Rory wants to play?"

Sully put his hand up for Jet to hold on a minute, and then he would explain.

Rory was a village constable. Actually, the only constable. Being a small village, not a lot happens there, and when Daria brought the Beast to town, these little races allowed them to blow the carbon out of their engines. At least, that was Rory's excuse. But Sully thinks he's taken a shine to Daria, and it gives him an excuse to see her.

She, on the other hand, thinks he's a pain in the ass, but as long as she gets to let the Beast off her leash without fines, she tolerates him.

"He said take your time, lass ... and be careful ... ya know, dhat ting scares the shite out of me!"

She laughed and said, "OK, Sully, see you in a bit." They hung up.

"Come with me." Sully waved for Jet to follow as he headed to the front of the pub.

They both stood at the window, waiting for something to happen. "Seriously, Sully, what's going on?"

"Hang on now ... listen, can ye hear dat?"

Jet nodded and looked at him like, what in the world?

Sully smiled. "It's da Beast!"

Both men stepped up to the window for a better view. The pub's silence shattered as the deep, guttural growl of Daria's solid black 1970 Challenger cut through the air. As the car rolled to a stop in the middle of the road, Daria's hand flicked the gear into neutral to let Rory and everyone within a mile radius hear the Beast awaken.

Rory's response was swift, his vehicle roaring to life, its lights flashing and siren wailing. But Daria, unphased, responded not with compliance but with a bold challenge—a single middle finger raised in defiance. Preparing for what was coming, she put it back in gear. Her foot slammed down on the accelerator as the Challenger's tires screeched in protest, gripping the blacktop, trying to claw its way forward.

Caught up by the moment's adrenaline, Rory launched his car into pursuit. Gravel spat out from under his tires, pelting the side of the pub as he tore away.

With a fierce jerk, Daria released the clutch, her car leaping forward, rubber burning, leaving a tale of rebellion imprinted on the road.

The race was on.

Screeching tires and roaring engines echoed through the air, and the smell of burning rubber filled Daria's nostrils as she pushed the Beast to her limits. The chase continued for miles as both cars disappeared out of sight, leaving behind a trail of dust and debris.

Jet stood, mouth agape. "That's hers?" Sully nodded. "Does this happen a lot?"

"Oh no, lad, not a lot. Just once a week or so."

"What?"

"I'm just joshin' ya lad." He patted him on the back and said, "It's gonna be a few minutes; let's grab a cuppa."

They were finishing their tea when they heard the Beast pull up. Both men returned to the front window by the door to greet Daria. Jet's gaze fixed on her as she stepped out of the car.

The scene that played in his mind was like something straight out of a rock music video in slow motion. Her movements were unhurried and graceful, allowing him to absorb every detail.

Her long, dark mahogany hair flowed in the wind, framing her face and highlighting her striking features. She wore a black cotton tee that hugged her curves perfectly, paired with a worn, matching leather jacket. Her hip-hugger leather pants accentuated her toned legs, and her biker boots gave her an air of confidence.

Daria's hips swayed slightly with every step she took, drawing his attention and making his heart race. She put her hands in her jacket pockets and sauntered up to the building.

Jet gulped hard as she got closer to the door. His palms became clammy, and his breathing quickened. Doubts began to flood his mind. *Shit, I can't do this! You have to do this... Fuck! Pull it together, man!* Remembering what was at stake, he took a deep breath, blew it out slowly, and with a renewed sense of determination, he pulled himself together and pushed forward.

Jet's phone rang as Daria stepped through the entrance; he turned away from the door. "I gotta take this, Sully." He tapped his phone and stepped away.

Chapter Ten

Panic at the Pub

(2021)

Daria walked into the pub and greeted Sully with a hug. He congratulated her on not dying in the Beast this morning.

She laughed. "Sully, I promise you, she's a tame beast. Besides, I drove much bigger and more dangerous vehicles than her on the farm."

He squeezed her a little tighter and rolled his eyes. "What am I gonna do wit ye, lass?"

As she looked around the pub to see the new owner, she caught his back as he was talking on the phone. She watched as he finished his call and turned to walk toward them.

Daria recognized him in an instant. The shape of his face, the curve of his smile, the eyes ... those eyes. She caught her breath and held it. For how long she couldn't tell, it didn't matter because it was already too late. She was already feeling her blood pressure drop, and the room started to spin. A cold sweat seeped through her skin, and tunnel vision began to set in as Sully introduced them.

Jet extended his hand to greet her, acting as if he didn't know her. Her hand, ice cold at this point, took his; it was all she could do ... finally, she breathed out, grabbed a quick breath in, and said, "Would you excuse me?" Then she walked into the kitchen.

She stopped in the middle of the counter, attempting to brace herself, but her body betrayed her, and she collapsed onto the floor, landing on her butt. Panic surged as she struggled to catch her breath. *What's happening? Why is it so hard to breathe?* Gasping and clutching at her chest. *Come on, dammit, get up. You need to get up!* With trembling hands, she grabbed the countertop and tried to stand, inadvertently knocking over a pot, which clattered loudly as it hit the floor.

Sully and Jet rushed through the door, alerted by the commotion, only to find Daria in distress. She was on the floor, legs crossed, rocking and holding her chest.

Jet reached her first, his movements swift as he knelt before her, gently lifting her face up to his. "Breathe, Lily," he told her in his most soothing voice. "Deep breaths. C'mon, babe, you can do this. Just breathe." Her eyes were closed in concentration as she followed his instructions, gripping his arms tightly.

Panting, she followed his lead, taking deeper and slower breaths until the raging storm within her calmed. Despite not having heard his voice in person since their last night together almost twenty years prior, his gentle words were still a soothing balm to her anxiety-ridden heart.

He held her face until she dissolved into tears. "You're here? How are you here?"

"It's okay, Lil, you're okay." He reassured her.

After what seemed like an eternity, their eyes finally met. Jet's heart skipped a beat as he saw the tears trail down her cheeks. Without a second thought, he tenderly wiped a tear away with his thumb, his touch lingering for a moment longer than necessary. Though giving her a reassuring smile, doubts still remained hidden deep within him.

Clutching his hand and holding it against her face, she buried her cheek into it. "I can't believe it's you. I thought I'd never see you again." Her voice, now trembling, panic rising again. "I'm sorry. I didn't know you were here. I just needed to come home." She looked up at him, her eyes pleading for understanding. "I didn't want to mess things up for you."

As he gazed into her eyes, filled with anguish and vulnerability, an overwhelming urge to comfort her washed over him. Every fiber of his being screamed for him to pick her up and hold her close, to kiss away her pain, and to never let her go. But beneath the surface, a whirlwind of conflicting emotions churned. Uncertainty clouded his thoughts, casting doubt on the feelings stirring within him.

What am I doing ... Jesus, it's as if nothing's changed; she breaks, and I come running.

Feigning strength, he offered reassurance, his voice steady despite the turmoil inside. "Hey, it's okay, you're okay." He didn't want to hear her apologies or see her tears; he needed to get away from her for a minute and to sort through his own emotions. "Okay, let's get you off the floor. C'mon now." He stood and pulled her to stand, then with his arm around her shoulders, he walked her to her room and sat her on her bed. "Why don't you lie down for a bit? You still look a little shaky."

This was his chance, his minute to think. "Listen, I have something I have to take care of, but I'll be back in a little while. Then we can talk."

He left her there on the bed with Sully nearby. Daria laid down and slept hard for about twenty minutes. When she awoke, Sully was at the desk. Sitting up, she found him walking over to sit next to her.

Jet had returned even more resolved to confront her and was about to enter her room when he overheard the two talking. His heart raced with a mix of anger and apprehension, unsure of what he might discover but still feeling compelled to find out. He stood outside the door, straining to catch every word, hoping she would give Sully some insight into why she was there.

Sully rubbed her back and asked, "Feelin' betta, lass?"

She nodded. "I'm sorry about all that. I don't know what happened."

"Looked like a foehll-blown panic attack to me, Love. I had no idea you two knew each other. Is he de one you've been hidin from all des time?"

She nodded. "So, I guess the cat's out of the bag, huh? It's been almost twenty years. I don't know what I was thinking or why I thought I could just come home and think things would be simple.

"When I returned to Leeds, I heard that he had gotten married. I didn't want to cause him any trouble, so I chose to find a small and secluded town where I could lie low and still be near my aunt. That's how I found you and this pub. I instantly fell in love with it! And as the saying goes, the rest is history!"

"I must ask dough, what brought ya back after all dose years, lass?"

"Sully..." She sighed, shaking her head. "It's a long and convoluted story."

"I've no place to go, lass."

Taking a deep breath. "Alright, well ..." She began to recount the twists and turns of her life story, from her troubled early days to the tumultuous move to England. Her words flowed like a river, and Sully felt moved by the current of her experiences.

"So, eventually, when I was sixteen, Jet and I decided to ignore the age factor and give our relationship a chance to see if it could work." Her eyes welled, and her voice shook. "And it did. It worked very well. He was the best part of my life for a while."

She got up to get a tissue. "When I was a few weeks away from being eighteen, my classes were finally over, and I couldn't wait to catch up to the band. They were still on tour through the rest of the summer, and Jet flew me out to meet them. It was insane, Sully. Travel during the day, concert at night ... party the rest of the night." She sat back down.

"On the night of the last gig, I went to the dressing room after the show and found Jet alone. He was just out of the shower and sitting in a chair wearing a towel and a pair of fuzzy bunny slippers I bought him as a joke. He was reading one of those music rags. I closed the door quietly behind me and locked it, and then, well, I won't go into detail, but suffice it to say I took advantage of the situation."

Jet remembered the night and thought to himself. *Yes ... yes, she did.* He couldn't help but smile.

Sully blushed a little, but continued to listen. "It must've happened that night because it was the only time we were actually alone on that tour until ... well, when we got home, it was busy. The boys were in and out of town for about six weeks or so, dealing with the record company, personal appearances, and interviews.

"Finally, things settled down, and we were able to return to a somewhat ordinary life. During that last weekend, we finally had some alone time. The rest of the guys were away, so I stayed at the flat with Jet. It started out perfect, spending almost every second in bed." Daria gave Sully a knowing look, and he smiled, understanding her confession.

"Anyway, I had a horrible dream Saturday night." She paused and looked away from him.

"Now that I think about it, I wonder if it wasn't some sort of premonition..." She laughed through her nose. "In my dream, I was walking through a room. It was so blindingly white that I had to squint to see anything. The room was featureless, with no visible walls, and even though I was alone, I felt trapped. I searched for a way out, but the more I searched, the more my panic grew. I could feel this overwhelming sense of doom or heaviness all around me. It was as if the room was expanding somehow, growing larger and more suffocating while I was getting smaller and smaller. Suddenly, I felt myself being yanked away from the light, and I started screaming uncontrollably, "Let us go! Leave us alone!" Jet woke me from my sleep and tried to help me calm down.

"When I woke up on Sunday morning, I took a shower and tried to analyze the dream.

"Back then, I thought it was about Jet and me being taken away or torn apart by something or someone. Humph, who am I kidding? I knew, or thought I knew, who it was..."

"Who, lass?"

"Rob—my stepfather, the one who all my nightmares were about. But now I believe this was a new set of dreams. These were about me and our unborn child being taken away.

"Jet being the ever-expanding light, my light, getting brighter and brighter as he and his band grew in popularity. And I was standing still. I realized, even then, at some point, I would have to be left behind. Not that I would have ever blamed him. I mean, it was what he and the guys had worked so hard for, ya know. Even now I have doubts about what I would've said to him. Would I have told him? Would he have given everything up to be a father? Would it have even been fair of me to ask that of him? I don't know. I guess it's a moot point now, doesn't really matter, does it? Because the following night, someone else made all those decisions for us.

She paused in thought, then returned to her original point. "But yeah, it was me and the baby who were being dragged away, for sure." She wiped her eyes with the tissue. "That was the first time that particular dream disturbed my sleep ... it creeps back every now and again when I'm stressed.

"At any rate, Jet and I went to his parents for brunch later that morning. While he and his dad talked in the parlor, I offered to help Mum in the kitchen. I told her I was late, like really late. And with all the excitement of the tour, I hadn't kept track of my period. And when I told her I might be pregnant, she was furious ... at first. Reminding me of all the times, she warned me to be careful and use protection. But we did, every time. I tried to tell her we were really good about that, ya know?

"After calming down, she reassured me that everything was okay, and we shouldn't worry until we found out for sure. She also told me about a store on the other side of town where nobody would know me, and you could purchase pregnancy tests without going to the counter and asking for them.

"It was early afternoon when we went back to the garage flat. They had a meeting scheduled, but as usual, it turned into a jam session. Later, when things settled down, I asked Jet if I could borrow his car to go to the store. He offered to take me himself; I think he just didn't want me driving his new car," she half laughed.

"So, when we got there and walked up to the store, Jet ran into an old schoolmate and started talking to him. I told him I was going in and I'd be right out. I followed Mum's instructions, went straight to the back of the store and found the tests on the back wall. I was reaching for one when someone grabbed me from behind. They put a cloth over my mouth, and the next thing I remember, I woke up in a car. Bound. My hands, my feet and my mouth. They put a cloth bag or something over my head because I couldn't see anything. I tried to get loose, but they drugged me again, and waking for the second time, I found myself sitting on the floor of an old cabin in the mountains of Kentucky."

Sully sat in shock. "Oh, lass, what did ye do?"

"Well, when I woke up, a young man was there. His name was Levi. He was cutting my ties as a sheriff came in, handed him our new IDs, and told us where to go. Evidently, I was Levi's new wife."

"What in da world?"

"Yeah, I tried to run once we got out of the cabin but ended up falling over a small cliff and hurting my knee. They brought a doctor to check me out, and that's when I found out I was, for sure, pregnant.

"I knew as soon as I had healed, I would try again to get away, but they were watching the house. During one of the visits with a doctor, I tried to get him to call my family. He agreed, but I never saw him again. I don't know how, but every. Single. Time. I tried to get away; they caught me.

"I tried so many times to escape, Sully. Once, I made it all the way to Atlanta, eight months pregnant, but there they were. They had the cops with them. One of the cops got on the bus to identify me and bring me to them, but I told him my story and gave him Jet's and my family's phone numbers. I almost had him convinced until his dispatch called the numbers and said that they were all disconnected. I couldn't believe it. It didn't make any sense.

"Needless to say, without any proof on my end he had to let them on. They literally tried to drag me off the bus, kicking and screaming. He didn't want me or the baby hurt, so he helped them hold me down while they sedated me, and I woke up in Kentucky again." She walked over to a window to look out and turned to him with tears streaming.

"I was too far along to try anything else, so I decided to just bide my time. I imagined it would be more complicated with a baby, but I told myself I would try again."

"I tried again a couple of years later when I felt the baby was old enough to run with. We made it to Utah that time. But yet again, we got caught. Sully ... I must have really pissed them off that time because they took the baby away from me after bringing me my grandfather's ear, for God's sake. They had always threatened to do things like that. But I never believed they would actually do it until they put it in a fucking box and had me open it like a Goddamn gift."

Disgusted, Sully cried, "God in heaven, who would do sucha din? So, what about des Levi boy? Was he any help?"

"No, unfortunately, I was his ticket out of jail. Evidently, he made some deal with a judge to marry Uncle's niece." She raised her hand. "That would be me. And if he stayed out of trouble, he wouldn't go back to jail. He turned out to be an abusive, raging alcoholic."

"What about this Uncle person?"

"So, Uncle was the man who actually took me. That was just the name he told me to call him. But, over the years, he and Jack got close."

"Jack?"

"Sorry, I'm trying to give you the condensed version. That's what I named our son; Jack is short for John."

"Des is all so…"

"I know, Sully … just another hopeless mess, right?"

"But how ded ye finally get away and make it back?"

"Well, Levi had been gone for years."

"Gone?"

"Story for another day." He nodded. "And the farm had always been Jack's home. He loved that place and wanted to turn it into a working dairy farm. So, I stayed for him. I figured that if I couldn't give him his father, I could at least give him a stable home and life. Then, when Jack was eighteen, we got a package in the mail.

"It contained all of my actual identification and a passport. It also had Jack's genuine birth certificate and a passport. And to top it off, the deed to the farm and all the properties surrounding it, along with a bank book containing a substantial amount of money.

"We used it to help Jack start the dairy farm with his new wife. I told him I'd stay till they felt comfortable running things, and when they got settled, he told me to come find his father. That I deserved some happiness, too."

"Yes, lass, dhat ye do."

"Well, that remains to be seen. With him being married now, I can only imagine how thrilled he must be at my reappearance. I mean, what are the odds I pick the one village in all the UK to hide out in, and it's right under his nose?" Sarcasm, heavy in her tone.

"Some would call dat fate."

"Or another unfortunate circumstance."

She sat beside him again. "Ahh, comb now, you dahn't believe dhat."

"Have you not been listening to my tales of woe? I swear, if I didn't have bad luck, I wouldn't have any luck at all." They both laughed.

Sully padded her on the knee and said, "Well, lass, I'm gahnna need a steffy if I'm to hear de rest of dis story."

"There's so much more, Sully, but that's the gist of it. I mean, he's here, I'm here … I guess it's up to him now. I'm tired, and I'm not going anywhere, even if he fires me. The UK is my home, too."

Jet stood still, his mind swirling with conflicting emotions after hearing her story. He couldn't wrap his head around what he had just learned. Part of him wanted to confront her immediately, but another part compelled him to verify the truth first. Determined, he turned on his heel and stalked out of the pub. Climbing into his car, he decided to confront his father instead, because things just weren't adding up. If everything she said was true, then he knew he had been right the whole time—especially when he remembered the last night of the tour she spoke of. An image slammed into his memory about that encounter. One he hadn't thought of since that night.

Chapter Eleven

Behind Closed Doors

(2002)

The concert had been electric. Every note, every cheer charged with an energy that left him with an abundance of adrenalin still coursing through his veins. But now, as the crowd's raucous approval faded into the background, all Jet could think about was seeing Lily.

Showered and lounging in a loose, soft robe, he tried to relax, skimming through a copy of *Rock Revival* magazine he'd picked up while waiting for the guys. They'd be walking in at any moment to get ready for the road trip home.

The metal handle to the dressing room door rattled and creaked open. His eyes followed her every move as she stepped inside, her presence instantly catching his full attention. The door snapped shut behind her, and with a soft, deliberate twist, the lock sent a subtle jolt through the air. The sound seemed to almost echo in the small room, speaking volumes—a signal that there would be no interruptions, no escape, and no turning back from whatever was about to unfold.

Lily's presence seemed to fill the space, and even in the dim light, he could see the flush on her cheeks. God, she was beautiful. It had been far too long since they'd been alone, and every part of him reacted instinctively, as if no time had passed at all.

She stood there for a moment, studying him. Her gaze lingered on the ridiculous bunny slippers he wore—slippers she had bought for him as a joke.

It made him smile despite himself. "Hey, don't judge, my girlfriend bought those for me," he said with a playful grin. His voice came out low, the sound of it like a magnet pulling her in.

Lily's smile curled up at the corners of her mouth. "She has shit taste," she teased, stepping closer.

Jet's gaze traced her every movement, lingering as though committing her to memory. His heart pounded, each beat echoing in his ears. She was close—so close—but not nearly close enough. The faint trail of her perfume, that familiar, intoxicating scent, filled the air, wrapping around him like a vise. It made his head spin, a cocktail of longing and anticipation. The tension between them thickened with every second, hanging in the charged air like a spark waiting to ignite.

"I thought we were going to meet on the bus?" he asked, trying to sound nonchalant, but his voice betrayed him. She took another step closer, and he wasn't sure how much longer he could keep his composure.

Lily didn't answer with words. Instead, she closed the gap between them, her fingers threading through his damp hair. He could feel the heat from her body as she straddled onto his lap. The closeness between them was electrifying, and for a moment, he simply let himself bask in it, her arms wrapping around his neck as she rested her forehead against his.

"I couldn't wait," she croaked, her voice barely above a whisper. "I needed to see you."

Jet's hands gripped her waist, holding her in place. "Well, now that you're here..." his nose nuzzled softly against hers. "I'm not letting you go," his voice was rough as he pulled her even closer, needing her more than he cared to admit.

"I was hoping you'd say that."

Lily's gaze softened, and then her lips were on his—slow, tentative, but building with intensity. He groaned as the kiss deepened, his grip tightening. Her scent, her taste, her warmth—everything about her consumed him. She was all he could think about, and now she was here, in his arms, where she belonged.

Jet's grasp tightened in a possessive pull, as if he was afraid she might disappear if he didn't hold on tight enough. They stayed like that for a few heartbeats.

When Jet finally spoke, his voice was rough with emotion. "I'm glad you came, Lil," he confessed. "Having you here with me means more than I can put into words."

"I'm glad too," she whispered, her voice thick with the weight of everything she hadn't said until now. "I was miserable while you were away."

Jet's heart clenched, his gaze softening as he brought one hand up to brush a strand of hair from her face, tucking it gently behind her ear. "Well, we're together now," he reassured, his thumb tracing the curve of her jaw.

The promise in his words sent a thrill through Lily, and she tilted her head, capturing his lips in a slow, tender kiss.

Jet responded immediately, his grip back on her waist, moving methodically downward until his hands were cupping each cheek, tightening as he squeezed, pulling her closer. Her skirt rolled up slightly, and he felt bare skin. He deepened the kiss, smiling against her mouth at his discovery and pouring all the unspoken words and pent-up desire into that moment.

About that time, they heard the handle of the door twist and grind, followed by a couple of loud bangs. It was Reggie and Ronny wanting in.

Jet sighed in exasperation as he released his grip. Lily locked her boots around the leg of the chair and whispered in his ear, "Let 'em wait." She pulled back from their embrace, giving him a wicked grin as she untied his robe. It fell open, revealing exactly what she had hoped to find—his fully erect member, standing at attention. Their eyes met, both hungry for the connection they hadn't been able to share since she flew out to meet him.

Lily came prepared. Pulling a foil packet from her bra that she got from the venue's restroom vending machine, she held it between her teeth as she took off her blouse, tossing it carelessly onto the floor. With practiced ease, she ripped open the packet and rolled the condom down his shaft, securing it with a downward stroke. Jet's head fell back, a groan of pleasure escaping his lips as his grip on her firm ass tightened. Lily raised herself up on one leg, positioning herself over him. As Jet entered her, an audible groan escaped both their lips, loud enough for the boys outside to hear.

Reggie was the first to complain. "Oh, come on, man!" He banged on the door a few more times, but Ronny just laughed, leaning back against the wall and crossing his arms, clearly amused by the situation.

Reggie glared at Ronny. "Don't get your panties in a wad, son. How many times have Jet and I stood outside waiting for you to get your rocks off with some backstage bint?" Reggie rolled his eyes, sliding down the wall to wait.

Inside, Jet and Lily had heard the commotion. And it was then when Jet decided there was no point in trying to be quiet. Lily's legs were too short to get any real momentum in that chair, so Jet just grabbed her ass and carried her to the wall by the door. She held tight to his neck, giggling and then laughing as they slammed against it.

Ronny felt the thud and stepped away from the thin wall, laughing even harder as he looked over at Reggie, who was now staring in disbelief. "Are you kidding me!" Reggie muttered, shaking his head with a grin.

For the next several minutes, the boys outside heard a series of crashes and thuds coming from the locked room. Jet had moved them from the wall, to the countertop, and then to the table. Creating a symphony of chaos as Lily's screams of pleasure and bursts of laughter echoed through the hallway. Even passers-by stopped to listen, their curiosity piqued by the ruckus coming from inside.

When Jet finally finished his tour of the dressing room, he was bent over Lily, who lay sprawled out on the table, her legs still wrapped around him. He kissed her deeply, both of them breathing heavily, their bodies slick with sweat.

Their eyes opened, finding each other's gaze. "Hey," Jet whispered, looking deeply into her eyes.

"Hey," she smiled, her voice filled with contentment.

"I missed you. I missed this."

"Me too."

Jet pulled away carefully, his movements tender as he helped Lily sit up. She adjusted her clothes, her cheeks still flushed from the dressing room workout. Meanwhile, Jet moved quickly, grabbing his jeans and slipping them on. As he removed the condom, he paused, frowning slightly.

It looked odd—stretched in a strange way, its shape uneven. He inspected it closely, turning it over in his hands. No visible holes or tears, but something about it didn't sit right. For a moment, a flicker of concern crossed his mind, but he shrugged it off when Lily spoke and broke into his thoughts.

"You good?"

Jet glanced at her, offering a reassuring smile. "Yeah, all good. You?"

"Mmm Hmmm."

Both continued to exchange playful, knowing glances. But Jet knew it was getting late, and they needed to get to the bus. So they finished dressing quickly. Then he grabbed Lily's hand and led her toward the door.

When he opened it, Ronny and Reggie were waiting in the hallway, staring in awe. Curious crew members had also gathered to see what the commotion was about. The looks on their faces were priceless—mouths agape, eyes wide with disbelief.

Ronny was the first to peek into the now-open room, surveying the wreckage left behind. "Damn, son," he chuckled, shaking his head in admiration at the shambles of the dressing room. Reggie, still seated, leaned around the corner to get a better look. "You trashed the place, man!" he laughed, glancing back at Jet and Lily, who were now walking away hand in hand.

The two looked back at each other and then burst into laughter, taking off running down the hallway like a pair of mischievous teenagers who had just gotten away with the ultimate prank. Their footsteps echoed through the corridor as the crew members exchanged amused looks, Ronny and Reggie shaking their heads in disbelief.

Chapter Twelve

Whatever it takes

(2021)

A week later, Jet drove home from his father's. It was late when he pulled up to the pub. Daria had already closed up, and the lights were out. He sat in the car, finishing a pint-sized bottle of whiskey, staring at the door, debating whether to go in or wait until morning.

At the same time, showered and in her fluffy robe and towel-dried hair, Daria hits the indoor pub light and heads to the kitchen for a snack before bed. As she sat at a booth to eat, the front door opened. Startled, she turned to see who it was.

Jet walked in and headed straight for the bar. He grabbed the first open bottle he found and two glasses. The smell of alcohol and cigarettes permeated the air as he walked past her, telling her he had already been drinking. He walked back to the booth, sat across from her, and poured them both a drink.

"I'll pay for the bottle."

"You already have; the place is yours, remember?"

"Yeah, I guess it is." He downed his drink and stared at her, not saying another word.

She's seen this stare before, he's pissed. *Why is he so pissed? If anyone should be pissed, it should be me. He blindsided me with the purchase of the pub and then just vanished. Where the hell has he been?* Seconds passed as he poured and downed another shot; she picked at her plate. *Well, whatever it is, it's gnawing at him; He looks like he needs to blow off some steam. Why doesn't he yell at me or something? I know it has to be about me being back. I guess I kind of ambushed him, too.* More seconds passed, along with another shot. *Dammit, Jet, say something! Yell! Scream! Fire me! Geez ... do ... something!* Even more seconds passed as he poured a larger shot, this time to finish the bottle. *Great! Now, he's finished the entire bottle ... maybe he should eat something.* She pushed her plate towards him to offer him some of her food.

He shook his head.

"It's yours too." Trying to pacify him.

With the most sarcasm he could muster. "I get it; everything in here is mine."

"Yep." She nodded as she downed her drink. *Well, that didn't do anything but provoke him.*

He took a deep breath, finished his drink, and then looked her in the eyes. "Does that include you?"

"You didn't buy me Jet; I've always belonged to you." *He has to know that.*

His eyes darkened into a wicked glint, and his lips narrowed into a thin line. As if to prove his ownership, he got up, moved to her side of the booth, and with a swift motion, grabbed the bottom of her robe, sliding her closer to him. The fabric of her robe whispered across the leather as he pulled her in. Burying his hand into her hair, he clutched her at the nape and pulled her head back, the scent of her shampoo—a sweet familiar floral—filling his senses. He claimed her mouth in a hard, bruising kiss, tasting the remnants of the alcohol they had just shared, then pushed her down onto the seat of the booth.

Umm ... okay ... I guess this is him blowing off some steam, she thought, her mind struggling to catch up with the sudden shift. *Hmmm ... this is ... uh ... not exactly what I had in mind ... but ... uh ... hmmm ... God, he tastes good.*

Her familiar sounds, soft moans escaping her lips, set him off like sparks to dry tinder, igniting a desperate need within him. He pulled open the top of her robe, the cool air brushing against her exposed skin, as he trailed lingering kisses and gentle nips down her neck. The sensation of his stubble scratching her skin sent shivers beneath his lips. Her hands instinctively grasped his head, sprawling her fingers through his unruly curls as he descended further. His breath, hot and ragged, ghosted over her chest as he gave equal attention to each breast, his lips soft but insistent, before continuing his journey downward.

The smell of her body wash—that hint of lilac, her favorite—wafted up, transporting him back to a time when that scent clung to him the rest of the night after dropping her off at her home. The memory, so vivid he could almost hear the echo of their laughter in the quiet of the pub.

It had been an eternity since the last time he felt her, the last time their hearts beat to the same rhythm. Savoring every inch of his downward trek, he let the anticipation build slowly as he guided her knees over his shoulders, the heat of her thighs pressing against his skin. His grip on her tightened, his fingers digging into the soft flesh of her thighs as he licked and sucked his way towards his intended target, leaving bruise-like marks as the blood pooled at the surface of her skin. He closed his eyes, anticipation building as he neared his target. Her familiar scent grew stronger, mingling with the raw, intoxicating scent of her arousal. Finding his mark, he teased her with each tantalizing lick and swirl of his tongue, feeling her body quiver in response, her breath hitching, as she echoed the unspoken yearning that lingered in him.

She gave in to his wanton need, her soft moans growing louder, more urgent, as he possessed her. Each sigh pulled him back to memories of shared moments and whispered promises that were never kept—promises he had longed for ... for so long. Why so long?

He intensified her arousal with his fingers, her muscles clamping down, sheathing around him, as he brought her to the precipice over and over again, only to stop, pulling back, leaving nothing but his hot breath just before she could cross the finish line. Her body trembled with frustration, her breath coming in ragged gasps, as he denied her release each time, hoping she would feel the same longing, the same ache of absence that had remained in him—his constant companion over the last twenty years.

He's punishing me ... he's definitely punishing me.

Daria lay spent, her body trembling, as he ended his final lap of carnal torture. She barely had time to catch her breath before he disentangled her legs from his grasp and seized the front of her robe, pulling her upright. He wrapped her arms around his neck, the searing heat of his skin pressing against her, and hoisted her onto the table, the wood cool and hard beneath her. His urgency was palpable in his deep and hurried kisses, his five o'clock shadow scraping her skin as he hastily unbuckled his pants. The sound of the metal buckle clanging against the wood echoed in the quiet room as he unleashed the next racer. Yanking her to the edge of the table, the sudden movement made her gasp as he found entry, and he leaned in once again to attack her neck, biting and sucking with a fervor that bordered on desperation.

With a forceful push, he drove her back onto the table; the impact jarring her, causing a sharp pain to shoot up her spine. He grabbed her arms, his grip like iron as he pinned them over her head, her wrists aching under the pressure. She couldn't move. Each thrust seemed to carry something different—something darker.

This wasn't him just blowing off steam anymore. This felt too familiar, and not in a good way. She felt trapped and scared, her heart pounding in her chest as the uncertainty of the situation became more unnerving. His vise-like grip around her wrists sent shooting pain through her, adding to the rising fear of where this was heading.

Okay ... this isn't fun anymore ... that hurts ... this needs to stop ... now!

"Stop!" she cried out, her voice strained. He ignored her, his eyes glazed over with something unreadable. Again, she begged, "Jet, please stop!" This time, her voice was filled with panic as she struggled to escape his grasp.

Jet's eyes became vacant, as though a light had gone out. He wasn't listening—he wasn't there. It was as if he had retreated into himself, devoid of recognition or understanding. Despite her struggle to fight against his control, he slammed her back down; the force ripping a cry of pain from her lips.

"Ow, fuck ... John ... Stop it!" she screamed, her voice shaking with agony and desperation as tears streamed down her face.

The sound of her using his given name jolted him like a thunderclap. He froze, a wave of shock washing over him. The weight of her sobs and the anguish in her voice shattered the haze in his mind, though he remained unsteady, teetering—one foot still lost in the storm, the other desperately searching for solid ground. His hands released hers immediately, and he staggered back, his face pale as the enormity of his actions began to dawn on him.

Lily pushed him away. She rolled off the table, her breath ragged. Her body froze as she tried to decide whether to confront him or retreat. Trembling, she steadied herself, pulling her robe closed, her eyes burning with anger and hurt. Without warning, she raised her hand and slapped him across the face; the sound echoing in the charged silence.

He didn't flinch, didn't move—he simply stood there, motionless, for what seemed like an eternity to Lily. Then, his chest heaved as reality hit him like a freight train. His eyes widened as he reached out for her.

"DON'T—" she choked, her voice breaking as tears spilled down her cheeks. But she couldn't finish. Shaking her head, she turned and stumbled toward her room, slamming the door shut behind her.

The reverberation seemed to shake the pub itself, leaving a heavy, oppressive silence in its wake.

"Fucking hell!" Jet cursed, his voice raw. His fist collided with the table, the wood groaning under the force of his frustration. Quickly pulling up his pants, he raced to her door, his heart pounding in his chest with a mix of madness and regret.

"Lily! Oh God, Lil, I'm sorry. Please," he pleaded, his voice cracking with desperation. He pressed his ear against the door, hearing the sound of her sobs through the thick wood.

"Lil, please let me in. Let me help you!" he begged, sliding down to sit on the floor. His head rested against the door, his fists clenched with remorse. Tears streamed down his face as he whispered, "Please ... I'm so sorry."

But no reply came. Only her muffled sobs reached his ears, amplifying the chasm between them. Each passing second of silence felt like another dagger through his heart.

At some point in the night, he must have gotten another bottle from the bar because it dropped onto the floor outside her door, making a clattering noise and waking her. She cracked the door to investigate, and Jet's limp body spilled into her doorway. He didn't wake, so she searched his pockets for his phone, and when she found it, she scrolled through it to find a familiar name.

"Yeah?" Thinking it was Jet.

"Reggie?"

"Lily? Is that you? Is everything okay?"

"Um, no, not really. I need someone to come get Jet. He's passed out, and I need to get the pub ready to open."

"I thought he was still at his dad's."

"Evidently, he came here on his way home. Could you just send someone for him, please? I gotta go."

Reggie and Ronny showed up a few minutes later to find Jet still on the pub floor.

"What happened?" Ronny asked. He could tell Lily had been crying and greeted her with a gentle hug.

"You'll have to ask *him* that."

They both looked at her as she pulled her collar up and hid her wrists from them with her robe and decided not to question her any further. Then, each grabbed an arm and got him out of the pub.

That afternoon, when Jet woke and found himself on his studio couch, he wondered, *How the hell did I get here ... the last thing I remember, I was ... shit.*

He got up, still confused, to check his security system, and saw that Ronny and Reggie had brought him in early that morning.

He rolled the camera footage from the pub back to the closing time and sat watching.

"Fuck! Fuck! Fuuuck!" he yelled, each one louder than the last, then kicked his chair back to stand.

Ronny was the first to hear him and quickly entered the room, followed closely by Reggie. Jet paced the floor frantically. "I fucked up, I fucked up! How could I do that!!" He turned back to them, tears running down his face, holding his head with both hands. The other two men caught a glimpse of the screen and walked over to see what he was talking about. They watched in disgust as Jet physically restrained Lily on the table as she cried and fought to get away from him.

"Dude, what the fuck!" Reggie exclaimed, turning to storm after Jet.

Ronny quickly intercepted Reggie, restraining him. "Hold on, man. Let's hear him out."

Reggie took a deep breath, collecting himself and pulling away from Ronny's grasp.

"What the hell were you thinking, Jet? Why would you do that?" Ronny's tone was calmer but still filled with outrage, his arms crossed tightly as he rubbed his temple with one hand. "Is she okay? Did you hurt her?" His voice dripped with concern and fury.

"I don't know, I don't know! I woke up here!" Jet pointed to the screen. "I checked the cameras to see how ... and found that!"

"Well, she seemed okay this morning. I mean, at least physically," Reggie interjected.

Both men gave Reggie incredulous looks, struggling to comprehend the situation.

"She was not okay, and you know it. And now we know why," Ronny retorted, his scowl deepening as he glared at Reggie before turning his attention back to Jet. "The question now is, what are you going to do about it?"

Jet grabbed his coat and ran out the door.

The pub was a buzz of activity when Jet got there. He walked in and sat in one of the booths. Daria was behind the bar wiping down some glasses when she noticed him. She poured him a pint, walked it over, and set it in front of him.

As he reached for her wrist, his gaze fell on the bruise forming around it. "Lily, I'm sorry. I don't know what happened. That wasn't me; I don't know who that was, but—"

Daria glared down at his hand and then back at him. He let go apologetically after noticing a rather sizable man, who had been observing their interaction, approach and position himself behind her.

Without acknowledging his words, she turned away from Jet and saw the big man.

"It's okay Liam." She patted his arm. "He owns the place."

Liam stood with his arms crossed, towering over Jet's seated position, holding his gaze. "That may be, love, but he doesn't own *you*."

Daria gave the man a sweet smile and then headed back behind the bar. Liam followed.

Jet sat in the booth all evening, watching her and waiting for her to finish up. Finally, she rang for last drinks, and the people finished up and slowly filtered out. When the last customer left, she locked up and continued to close the place down.

When she finished, she approached him and asked, "Do you have your keys?"

He pulled them out of his pocket, thinking that she needed them. "Yes."

"Lock up when you're done." Then she turned, walked to her room, and locked the door behind her.

She got into the shower, letting the warm water wash the day away. Remembering the night before, she tried not to let those feelings of anger and humiliation roll through her already troubled mind.

This was a man she loved and respected. Hell, he basically helped raise her. How could he do something like that to her? The word "betrayal" echoed in her mind, evoking the same feelings she experienced whenever her stepfather, Rob, or Levi had attacked her. How was she going to let this go? How was she going to forgive him?

The next morning, as she emerged from her room, she found Jet still sitting in the booth, fast asleep. In the morning sun's light, his face appeared more gentle, and pausing momentarily to drink him in, she couldn't help but notice how the passing years and lifestyle choices had taken a toll on him.

There was a vulnerability in his slumber, and his once smooth features now seemed a bit more weathered. The fine lines etched around his eyes and mouth spoke volumes, hinting at the battles he must have fought within himself.

The beautiful boy who had flounced down in front of her all those years ago was still in there, somewhere, and she couldn't help feeling a twinge of pity for him, especially since she didn't know what struggles he had been through over the last twenty years.

Despite her inner turmoil, she was only fooling herself, and deep down she knew her heart would eventually forgive him. But forgiveness was not something she thought she was capable of just yet.

Not wanting a confrontation at the moment, she went to the kitchen and started a kettle. Leaning against the counter, she found herself lost in thought, her mind churning with everything that had occurred over the past few days, each detail dissected and analyzed until it felt like she was, as they say on the farm, beating a dead horse.

When the kettle was ready, she poured each of them a mug, prepared it the way she remembered, and then sat in the booth across from him. She pushed the hot mug of tea in front of him, and he woke up. He lifted the hot drink to his face, letting the steam wash over him.

As he took a quick sip, he glanced over his mug to see her watching and waiting for him to say something.

When he didn't, she spoke first, "Are you ready to try this again, or did you just come by for another grudge fuck?"

"Don't be so crass, Lily," he croaked.

She looked at him like, *really*, then got up and walked away.

"Lily, please. I want to talk."

Turning back slowly, and again sitting down in front of him. She waited, then raised her eyebrows.

After another moment of silence, he finally said, "First off, I owe you an apology for what happened the other night. I should've just left and talked to you later, but when I saw the light come on ... I had to see you. I can't really explain it, I just had to ..." He paused for a beat, studying her reaction, then added with a smirk, "Why didn't you kick my ass? I've seen what you can do here at the pub. You could've easily taken me down in my condition."

She locked eyes with him, her expression steely. "Let's get something straight," she said, voice low and steady. "I could take you on any day—no matter the condition. But that day ... that wasn't a good day, for either of us."

He pursed his lips. "You're right, but still. Why—"

"Because you needed it."

When she said that, he was taken aback.

And there it was: immediate forgiveness. She let it slip sooner than she had expected, but she couldn't let him take all the blame because she wanted him that night as much as he needed the release.

"You left. You were gone, and I didn't know if you were ever coming back. And when you did, you were … well, I could tell you were upset because you weren't talking. So, when you came at me, I thought maybe you needed to just blow off some steam. I thought maybe it would help you get through whatever was bothering you.

"And if I'm being completely honest, I needed to feel your touch, too. I just didn't … I let it go too far, and you …" She took a long, shaky breath. "I could see it in your eyes; you weren't there. You were somewhere else and so angry. I didn't think you were going to stop. And that's when I got scared. The whole thing was my fault. I should never have—"

"Lily, stop!" He slid out of the booth and dropped to his knees in front of her, locking his hands around her waist, pulling her close. He squeezed her tight, his voice thick with emotion as he struggled to keep it together. "I'm sorry. I fucked up. It wasn't you I was pissed at. Well, maybe at first, yeah. But not now … I was just so damn confused when you came back."

He paused, his grip tightening around her. "I didn't know why you were here, and after the way you left, I didn't want to risk getting hurt again. Losing you almost destroyed me the first time, Lil. Tell me what to do. I'll do whatever it takes to make this right. You know I'd never hurt you on purpose. I couldn't live with myself if I thought—"

She reached down, her touch gentle as she lifted his chin, guiding his face toward hers. Daria's lips pressed to his in a kiss that was as tender as it was forgiving. It was a kiss that said everything Jet needed to hear, a forgiveness that words couldn't do justice to. In that moment, everything he'd done wrong seemed to fall away. She was forgiving him.

He rested his head against her chest, his arms still wrapped around her, holding on like he was afraid she'd slip away. His voice was low, filled with frustration and vulnerability. "I've been so fucked up since you got back. My head's all over the place."

He sighed heavily, his breath shaky. "I came back that day to confront you. I was about to walk into your room, but when I heard you talking to Sully, I stopped. I stood outside your door, listening to the pair of you. It wasn't easy hearing that shit, but I had to. I needed to know if you were being real. When you were done, I bailed. Went straight to Pops to see if he could back up what you said."

She tightened her embrace around him, laying her cheek on his head, feeling his despair and remorse.

"Lily, the whole horrible ordeal. Every damn thing you went through all those years and I wasn't there for you. I didn't protect you."

"Don't say that—"

There was a long, agonizing silence as Jet fought to hold it together. "I can't believe I have a kid."

"Yes, you do, John. And he's incredible. He's a good man, you'd be proud of him." She lifted his face toward hers, trying to ground him, bring him back. "You're a good man," she whispered, her eyes glistening with tears as she met his gaze.

He shook his head, his voice rough. "I'm not a good man, Lily. You don't know the guilt I've carried since you disappeared. A good man wouldn't have let you go off alone. I should've kept you with me, held your hand, made you stay until we walked in together. I'm sorry for everything that happened to you because I let my guard down. I knew something was off, I couldn't believe you'd just haul ass like that."

She stared at him, her expression soft but resolute. "Jet, how could you have known that was going to happen? Hell, I felt perfectly safe walking in by myself that night. It's not like I was a child."

Jet gave her a side-eyed glance, knowing the history between them. "Maybe you weren't a kid, but—"

"Okay, okay, I might've looked like one, but still," she remarked, remembering that even Levi thought she looked like a child at the time.

"We searched everywhere that night. The band, all our friends—we all went out looking for you. We even called 999 and got the police involved. Mum and Pops went to talk to your family. They found your diary, Lily. Your words ... you wrote about us, about how you were unhappy, about wanting to leave for the US."

"Wait, I never kept a diary. I never wrote to anyone."

"I know that now. But back then, I didn't know what to believe. Our families—they tried to convince me you were gone for good. They said you didn't love me anymore. But I didn't buy it. I kept searching for you. I looked for you at every gig, in every crowd, in every town. Your face haunted me, Lil. Everywhere I went, I'd see a flash of your brown hair and think it was you."

He sank back on his knees, releasing his grip on her. She gently wiped the tears from his face, the back of her knuckles tender against his skin. "Neither one of us is to blame. Someone did this to us."

Jet nodded as he released a heavy sigh. "Lily, when I heard that you told Mum that you might be pregnant and she never said anything to me about it, I was so fucking angry. I couldn't believe it. I talked to Pops, and he told me he thought Mum's family might've had something to do with your kidnapping."

"What? No … it was Rob, it had to be … the constant threats. I figured he finally found a way to get back at me and Grandpa."

"Lily, Rob was killed well before you were taken. He was shot by the police in some sort of raid. Anyway, it couldn't have been him."

"How do you know all this?"

"That's what I came to talk to you about that night. While I was home, Pops showed me a stack of boxes Mum had hidden away. It was overwhelming—so much that it took me almost the entire week just to get through one box.

"And there's still more. A lot more, Lily, and you need to see it. I couldn't believe half of what I was reading—the lies, the deception. It's bigger than I ever imagined, and that's why I was so angry. Not at you. I've never been able to stay cross with you, you know that. I was hoping you'd come back home and go through it with me. I need your help—it's way bigger than I can handle alone."

"What about the pub?"

"Fuck the pub!"

"You're right, of course."

"I'm sorry. I know how much this place means to you; maybe I can get Sully to take it over until we get back," she nodded and placed her hand on his chest in agreement.

He took her hand, pressing it against his cheek. His lips brushed her palm, soft but deliberate. "Lily," he said, his voice low and steady, "I've loved you for as long as I can remember. I've missed you every bloody day since you left. You were everything to me—more than my best mate, more than family. You were my world, even before I knew it. My confidant, my anchor... and then my heart. My whole damn heart. I screwed up. I know I did. But, Lil, you need to know—I never stopped loving you. Not for a second. Please, just ... forgive me."

Her eyes softened, and she shook her head. "There's nothing to forgive," she said, her voice quiet but firm.

As their lips met in a kiss filled with compassion, a rush of emotions flooded through them both. Yet, amidst the whirlwind of their rekindled connection, lingering questions remained unanswered, along with secrets yet to be unveiled.

Chapter Thirteen

Everybody Lies
(2021)

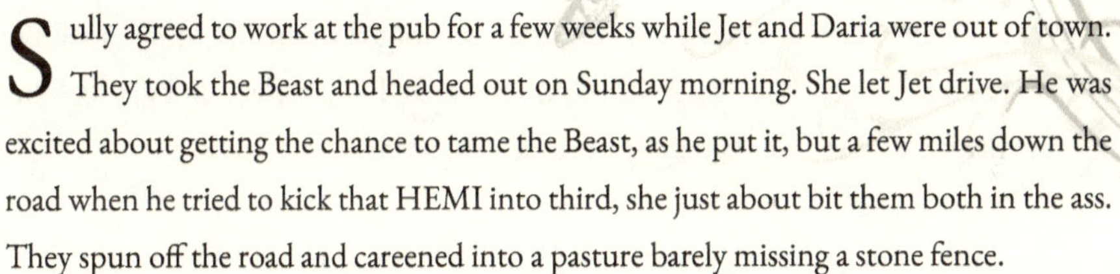

Sully agreed to work at the pub for a few weeks while Jet and Daria were out of town. They took the Beast and headed out on Sunday morning. She let Jet drive. He was excited about getting the chance to tame the Beast, as he put it, but a few miles down the road when he tried to kick that HEMI into third, she just about bit them both in the ass. They spun off the road and careened into a pasture barely missing a stone fence.

Grabbing the dash with both hands, she questioned, "Are you sure you can handle her?"

He tried to make an excuse. "Of course I can! We must've hit a slippery spot in the curve back there!"

"Babe, this ain't one of your little Italian high-performance cars. The Beast was built with muscle for speed, not maneuverability. She's a tank! Think quarter mile, not Indy Car; you can't take those curves like that."

After getting the Beast back on the road, he finally looked at her and flashed a big smile before saying, "Let's give it another go, shall we?" The tires spun out, slinging mud onto the road behind them.

She rolled her eyes, shaking her head. "You're washing her! Now, let's try to get there in one piece, please."

They pulled up to Jet's parents' home unscathed and walked in to greet his father. Pops met them at the door. He stepped past Jet, grabbed Lily, and held her tight for a long moment. "Oh, Lily girl, I've missed you!"

Teary-eyed, she hugged back, kissing him on the cheek. "Me too, Pops."

"Come in, you two. We've set some lunch out for you."

Since Mum passed, Jet hired a care person to come in and help Pops with meals and tidying up. She greeted them as they came in and sat at the kitchen table. "Thank you, Ana," Pops said as he sat.

They took their bags upstairs to unpack when they finished with lunch. Jet went to his old room, and Lily walked past him to the guest room. He looked at her like, where are you going?

She caught his glance, dropped her bags onto the bed, then walked back to him.

"We're gonna need to discuss your marital status, babe. I'm not a side chick."

His following expression was, Oh shit, I almost forgot about that. Lily raised her eyebrows and went back to the guest room. He walked in after her and grabbed her around her waist from behind, pulling her into a tight hug.

"I'm serious, Jet."

"But, at the pub, you let me —"

"That was therapy."

"I'm feeling like I may relapse at any moment, though."

"The doctor is no longer on duty ... and until further notice, she's on sabbatical."

He stooped down, nuzzling his face into her hair, feeling the silky strands brush against his skin as he inhaled deeply, savoring her familiar scent—a mix of floral shampoo and her natural essence that always drove him wild. His breath lingered, hot against her ear, as he whispered in a low, seductive voice, "You know you want me."

Then, with deliberate slowness, he trailed his lips down to the curve of her neck, where he knew her most sensitive spot lay waiting. His lips brushed against her skin, soft and moist, before he bit down gently, sending a jolt of electricity through her that made her breath catch in her throat.

Every pore on her body pricked as she melted inside, wanting to turn around and give him the response he begged for. *Fuck me ... no dammit, that's exactly what we don't want ... right?* She lied to herself, trying to ignore his advances.

She did her best not to respond, so he let go and sulked out of the room.

The day passed as they sat with Pops, filling him in on Lily's whereabouts while reminiscing about the old days. Mum had always been pretty tight-lipped about her past with Pops, and he never pushed her to reveal more. All he knew was that she had left home at a young age, and that's when they met.

The following day, they were ready to get to work going through the papers. Jet picked up a box and set it on the kitchen table. Lily grabbed another and opened it up to go through it. "So, this is where I left off. This box is the only one I've gone through so far. From what I could piece together, we are descendants of these clans from Romania."

"Gypsies?" she asked.

"Maybe?"

"What do they say? How do you know you're related to these clans?"

He pulled out one of the files and opened it, showing her, "This file has a birth certificate or birth record for me and every male in my family, going back generations. They are all from Romania. I was born here in the UK ... I'm not sure why I have one from there unless it means I may have dual citizenship?" He shrugged, then asked, "Do you remember your biological father, Lily?"

"No, my mom never really talked about him. I just assumed that he was one of her many flings. I was little when Grandpa got custody, remember?"

"Well, there's one in here for Emil Daniel. I know your last name is Daniels ... too close to be a coincidence, don't ya think?"

"Huh ... I know my family is Eastern European, but no one ever discussed it. Grandpa and Uncle Abe still had their Romanian accent; that's how I recognized the man who took me was Romanian."

"Well, most of these documents in this box are about Mum's family.

"There's some stuff in here about Uncle Andrei, Mum's brother, and properties he owns in the US and eastern Transylvania along the border of Moldavia ... I know he lived in the States and made his money there, but according to some of these documents, he used his money to buy land in Romania to set up villages for the clan."

Lily was looking through a file as he talked. "Hey, Jet?"

"Hmmm?" Concentrating on his file.

"Do you remember that girl you went to Liverpool with ... for the weekend... ya know, the one whose dad took the whole band to see that club?"

"You mean the girl you threw a fit over?"

She jokingly sneered, "Yeah, yeah ... What was her name?"

"Gemma, they moved shortly after that. Why?"

"Hang on ..."

Lily picked up another file, flipped through it quickly, then another and another ... she displayed them side by side on the table, "Gemma, Sarah, Lorna and a bunch of others here that I don't recognize, but you might."

He walked over to her side of the kitchen table to see as Lily grabbed another box to sift through. "What the hell? Are these all the girls I ever dated? Holy Hell Lil?" He grabbed the box and finished flipping through the files. "Geez, I don't even remember her. Wait, they even have Gabriella in here. Each one is like some kind of dossier of their lives."

He started going through them even faster, looking for something. "How come you're not in here?" He looked over at her as she looked at a file from a third box.

Lily sat still, looking at a page in one of the files she pulled from the new box, then flipped through the box, glancing at the rest of the files. "Because I have an entire box to myself, it seems." She looked up to greet his eyes, both in a state of shock.

Then, at the same time, they yelled, "POPS!"

Pops entered the kitchen; both Lily and Jet were staring at him. "What?"

Jet started. "Did you know about any of this?"

"Son, your uncle brought all these boxes the last time he visited us. And then, after your mother died, I had no idea what they were or why they had them. I put them up in the spare room and looked through some of it; and what I saw, I decided I didn't want to know anymore. So, I left them there until I could figure out what to do with them. I guess I just never got around to it. When you came home asking questions, that's when I remembered they were here."

"Pops, how did you meet Mum?" Lily asked.

Frank sat in a chair, a soft smile tugging at his lips as he lit a cigarette. "We were young, around eighteen at the time. She had just moved here from Poland—came to Leeds on her way to London. She was sitting in this little cafe across the square, one of those places where the coffee is so strong it could wake the dead." He chuckled, shaking his head. "I saw her there, sitting by the window, all serious and quiet, with her hair pulled back and this little notebook in front of her. She looked ... well, like nothing I'd ever seen. I was mesmerized."

Lily grinned. "Did you just march right up to her?"

"Not exactly," he admitted, smirking. "I watched her for a while from across the square, pretending to be reading the paper like some secret agent." He laughed, the sound gravelly. "When it seemed like no one was meeting her, I finally worked up the nerve to go over.

She looked at me like I was mad when I asked if I could join her. But she didn't say no. Her English wasn't great—she knew just enough to get us through that first conversation, mostly smiles and hand gestures. But even then, there was something about her, you know? Like we understood each other without needing too many words.

"We met again the next day. And every day after that. I showed her around Leeds—what little of it there was worth showing back then—and we talked about everything. She told me a little about her life in Poland. I told her about mine. And somewhere in those weeks, she decided to stay here instead of going on to London. Best decision she ever made, if you ask me." He winked.

"So why did you wait so long to have Jet?"

He sighed, rubbing the back of his neck. "We didn't want to wait, hun. We tried for years. But back then, they didn't have all this modern technology—no IVF, no fancy treatments. Just hope and prayer. At some point, we gave up on trying. Thought it wasn't in the cards for us. And then, one day, out of the blue, we found out she was pregnant with John. A bloody miracle, that one."

Jet smiled at his father and Lily half laughed and said, "Yeah, that's usually how it happens. I ask because I was wondering if you could give us some insight into who any of these people are from Mum's side of the family? There are a bunch of names in here, but we don't know any of them."

"I'm sorry, Love, but the only people I ever met were Andrei and his wife."

"So then, what made you think Mum's family had something to do with my kidnapping?"

"The box that Jet opened was the first one I looked at, too. When I saw that her family was Romanian, not Polish, something clicked. And when Jet told me some of what had happened to you, a documentary I once watched came to mind. It was about the Roma Gypsies and the persecution they faced during the Holocaust. The Nazis targeted them alongside Jews and others they deemed undesirable, with hundreds of thousands killed or dying from the horrific conditions in concentration camps. Despite these horrors, many Roma families escaped to other countries, determined to preserve their culture and rebuild their lives.

"What stood out to me wasn't just their suffering—it was their deep dedication to family and their respect for cultural traditions, particularly surrounding marriage. In many Roma communities, marriage wasn't just about two individuals; it was a way to unite families and preserve their heritage.

"What kind of traditions?" she asked.

"Child brides and bride kidnapping."

Lily paused, processing the weight of it.

"Some of those customs had a pretty dark side," Frank continued. "For instance, bride snatching was a practice in some Roma groups where a man could kidnap a woman he wanted to marry or make a forced alliance with her clan. Sometimes it was consensual, akin to an elopement, but often it wasn't, and the woman had little choice. It was seen as a demonstration of the man's determination and, in most cases, was later legitimized by her family. While it's rare today, the practice may still occur."

Frank added, "When I thought about all this after looking at those papers, I couldn't help but wonder—could Mum's family, or someone from her past, have engaged in some of these traditions? Even the darker ones?"

Jet and Lily exchanged suspicious glances with one another. "Yeah, but they didn't marry me off to another Romanian."

"Are we sure? I mean, they took you to America. Could the boy have been of Roma descent? It's just that so many things from the show fit your situation and sounded like some of the scenarios in the documentary. And even if he wasn't Roma, you said your kidnappers were ... could they have just been doing what came naturally to them and their culture?"

"Hmm ... interesting thought. He didn't look Roma, but ... well, there's still a lot to go through. Maybe something else will give us some clues. Jet, are there any pictures in that first box?"

"Yeah, loads."

"Okay, let's just work one box at a time." She packed up all the boxes except for the first one Jet and his father started on. "Now, where are the files with the earliest dates? Let's lay them out chronologically."

When they finished, they stood back and looked at them.

Pops said, "It almost looks like a family tree."

"I think you're absolutely right. What's the date on that first folder, Jet?" Lily said.

"1820."

"Who's in it?"

"Bartholoways Marin."

"Who's next?"

Pointing at each file as he spoke. "All of these have the same surname, so this is Tamas 1837. Then, Milosh 1856, Luca 1874, Beskin 1896, Andrzej 1918 ... and lastly, we have Mum's father, Stefan, in 1936 and Uncle Andrei in 1953. Then me, last name Thomas, in 1978. The only other outliers are these two, Emil Daniel 1943 and Marik Daniels 1968."

"Pull any pictures that match the names and dates, then attach them to the top of the folder. I'm gonna run up and grab my laptop." She left to go upstairs while Jet and Pops got to work. When Lily returned, she tried to find more information about the names online but unfortunately had no luck. When Jet and Pops were done, she walked over to see the files, and the attached pictures.

Andrzej, Stefan, Andrei, and Jet were the only files they could match with photos.

Lily smiled as she picked up and opened Jet's file. She teased, rubbing the picture with her finger. "Such a sweet baby."

Jet grinned and shook his head. She looked through it and found the basics: date of birth, where, what hospital, etc. She put it down, already knowing most of his history, and picked up Andrei's.

Lily stood still, staring at the picture. Jet and Pops noticed a definite change in her demeanor. "Lily? Love, are you okay?" Pops asked.

Jet walked to her side and put his hand on her shoulder. His touch brought her back. "This is your uncle?"

"Yeah."

"This is the man you say you saw the night I went missing?"

"Yeah, he said he was here on a layover from a business trip and headed back to the airport. Why?"

She pulled the picture off the folder and laid it on the table for them to see. "This man, along with another, took me that night."

Pops grabbed the back of the chair nearest him to steady himself.

Jet rushed to help him sit, then looked back at Lily. "Are you sure?"

"Jet, I just spent the better part of twenty years with this man. Hell, the first several I spent trying to get away from him. After Jack was born ... Well ..."

"Well, what?"

"Listen, I'm telling you I know this man. We called him Uncle. That's what he told us to call him ... I guess at least that part was true."

Pops spoke up, "It makes sense, son. He was there at the store, you said. Right?" Looking at Jet. "You saw him and spoke to him. He was rushed and told you he was headed for the airport."

"It must've been the Brit, Giles, who drugged me inside and took me to the car," Lily said.

"Lily, there's no way. I've known this man all my life. He wouldn't do something like that. You have to be mistaken."

She opened the file to see more pictures confirming to herself that Andrei was indeed Uncle. Then she grabbed the pictures from the box and started going through them. She laid all the photos she recognized people in on the table. She stopped at one and immediately teared up. "What is it?" Jet begged.

She slammed the photo onto the table and ran out of the kitchen.

"Lily, where are you going?" Jet called after her, his voice tinged with confusion.

By the time he reached the stairs to follow her, she was already on her way back down, a book clutched tightly in her hand. She passed him without a word; he followed her back into the kitchen, a knot forming in his gut.

When she returned to the table, she picked up the picture and showed it to them both. "Who is this boy?" she demanded, her voice barely steady.

Pops looked at the photo, his face crumpling with a mix of recognition and sorrow. "My nephew," he said, his voice thick.

Jet's throat tightened. "My cousin."

Lily opened the photo album. She flipped through it with an urgency that made Jet's heart race.

She stopped at a series of pictures, each one showing Jack around the same age as the boy in the photo. She turned the album so both men could see, her eyes brimming with unshed tears. "Your son," she whispered.

Pops let out a choked sob, his hands shaking as he buried his face in them. Jet just stood there, his mind reeling, unable to process the weight of the revelation.

"Do you know what this means?" Lily said.

Jet sank into a chair next to Pops, unable to respond. He stared at the album, at the boy who was his son, trying to absorb the truth that had just shattered everything he thought he knew.

"How often did you get to see him, Jet?" Lily asked. "Hey!"

Pop answered for him, "Andrei brought him to see us a few times a year. Mum made sure John was home to see him, too. She said our family was small, so spending time together and seeing one another whenever possible was important."

Lily moved closer, her presence comforting as she sat next to Jet. She stroked his arm, grounding him, then took his hand in hers, their fingers intertwining. He looked over at her, his vision blurred with tears he hadn't realized had started to fall.

"You got to see your boy grow up." She smiled through her tears. Her chest ached realizing that yet another lie had been revealed. "I know it's not the same as raising him, but ... my biggest regret was that you never got to meet him ... and it turns out ..." Jet pulled her into a tight embrace, holding on to her like his life depended on it.

After what felt like an eternity, he let go of her. Lily put her hand on his cheek, her reassuring touch soothing him as she wiped a tear with her thumb. Finally, she sat back and picked up Andrei's file. "Pops, I don't know how much you knew or suspected over the years, but ... Jet, your uncle was not the man you thought he was."

She hadn't told them everything. Initially, she didn't think it was relevant, but it was evident now that they needed to hear more of her story.

She took a deep breath contemplating her next statement, then, with a heavy sigh, she explained, "After Jack was born, he was around two when Uncle, or rather, Andrei, took him for the first time. I lost my shit. I thought he was taking him from me as a punishment for trying to run again. I told him that if it took me the rest of my life, I would find a way to kill him. And at that moment, I was serious. I attacked him physically. It took Giles and Levi to pull me off him."

She stood and walked around the table to address them both from a distance so she could read their mood as she continued, "When they dragged me off of him, Giles and Levi had me pinned to a chair. The doctor took Jack and left the house while Andrei stood in front of me, wiping his bloody face with his handkerchief. He was smiling. It was the weirdest thing. He just stood there, nodding and smiling. I remember him saying under his breath as he walked out of the house, 'She'll do.' I didn't know what he meant by that until he brought Jack back home to me."

Lily walked to the sink, picked up a glass from the dish drainer, and filled it with tap water. She drank about half of it, staring out the window over the sink while the two men waited, then turned to continue.

"A few weeks later, the doctor came to the house and picked me and Jack up. She brought me to this facility on the other side of the mountain. It was like a warehouse, but they had it converted into this scary gym of sorts. Not like regular workout equipment, but like … it was sectioned off to simulate places; one corner was a house, and another corner was set up as an office. Another area was a gun range, and of course, gym equipment scattered around, but it was like they were training for some kind of, I don't know, James Bond crap.

"Anyway, Andrei sat me down and told me if I was going to kill him, I'd better be better at it than him. I looked at him in disbelief and told him he was crazy, that I was just angry when he took Jack, and he said I showed promise, and he wanted me to train with his people.

"I told him that I was a girl, not a gangster. He thought that was funny and said, 'Is that what you think of me?' I said, well, given our history. He nodded and said, 'Yes, I can see how you might think that.' Then, he assured me he was nothing more than a businessman but that he liked protecting his assets. I asked if Jack and I were assets and he thought for a second and then responded with, 'My most precious.' I didn't know how to react to that."

She stopped to allow Pop and Jet to respond, but both men sat stone-faced, staring at her.

"Anyhow, I didn't initially take him up on the offer. Even though it would have given me a bit more freedom and time away from Levi, I couldn't bear to be away from Jack. Later, though, as he got older and didn't need me as much, he asked again. I told him I would think about it. It wasn't until … well, there was an incident with Levi, and I felt I needed to learn how to protect myself and Jack."

That caught their attention. "What kind of incident?" Jet insisted.

Lily cocked her head and stared at him for what seemed like a little too long until Pops got up. It looked like he needed to leave the room. Lily figured he knew exactly what she was talking about, but couldn't bear to hear the words.

The entire situation already had him rethinking his whole life and marriage to a woman he evidently knew nothing about; she figured this would just break him. He stood waving his arms as if to say no more, then he turned to leave, shaking his head, visibly upset. Lily couldn't tell if he was holding back a wail or an obscenity, but he kept it in long enough to shuffle out of the kitchen and into the parlor.

"One I don't care to relive at the moment. It was a long time ago, but needless to say, I needed to be ready in case it happened again."

"Lily?" His voice softened with concern as he leaned forward. "Did he hurt you? Did he hurt Jack?"

She let out a bitter laugh through her nose. Her eyes blinked away from him, focusing on something distant, something painful. "He hurt me a lot … but that was just …" She shrugged, the motion almost mechanical, like she was shaking off an unwanted memory. "a regular day for him."

Her words hung heavy in the small kitchen.

"Then, what, Lily? What did he do? What made you decide?" He pushed.

Angry tears pricked her eyes, and she croaked, "You're gonna make me say it! You can't just take my word? You want to hear all the gory details of the night he came home drunk off his ass and saw me watching you on the TV, singing *my* song, and got so enraged that he kicked in the television and then raped me while Jack watched. Is that what you want to hear?"

She broke and turned away.

"Jesus, Lil!" In an instant, he was by her side. His arms, the same powerful arms that had always protected her from her nightmares, that had picked her up when she fell, the same arms she had once slept in, now wrapped around her body, pulling her tight against him. Her face buried into his chest, and she breathed in deeply, the familiar scent of him—a comforting mix of warm musk, faint cologne, and something uniquely him—washed over her, grounding her in the present moment. *Oh God, I need this; I need him*, she thought, feeling the tension in her body slowly unraveling.

"No, I'm sorry. I wasn't thinking. I didn't realize that he… Shit. And then when I … Oh God Lil, I'm so sorry," he murmured into her hair, his voice thick with regret. He pressed a tender kiss to the top of her head, and they swayed together.

Lily tightened her grip around his waist, her fingers curling into the fabric of his shirt, letting the soothing closeness of his body ground her.

"I think we need a break," he whispered. She nodded, the movement small and almost imperceptible, her face still pressed against him, unwilling to let go just yet.

Chapter Fourteen

It was Time

(2021)

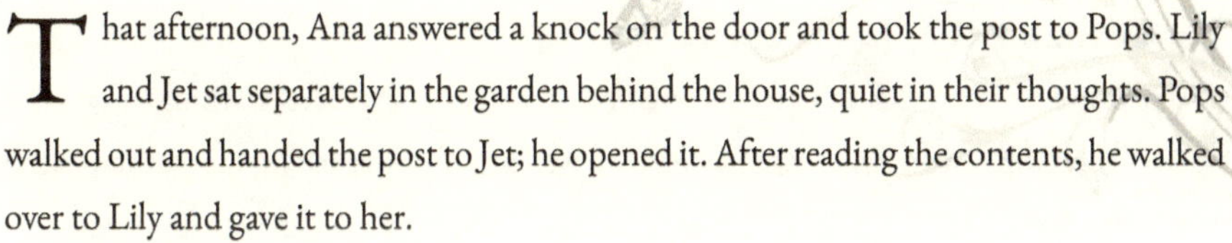

That afternoon, Ana answered a knock on the door and took the post to Pops. Lily and Jet sat separately in the garden behind the house, quiet in their thoughts. Pops walked out and handed the post to Jet; he opened it. After reading the contents, he walked over to Lily and gave it to her.

"What's this?"

Jet gestured for her to read it. She flipped through the file and looked up at him.

"Divorce papers? When did you do this? I mean, I don't understand?"

"That first night, when I saw you in the pub, I knew I needed to file for divorce. It's been coming for a long time, but I just couldn't be bothered with the hassle. It didn't matter whether or not it was you. This marriage was a farce. She doesn't love me, and I never loved her. I'll sort her a generous settlement and be done with it. Besides, I'm fairly certain all those trips to London to 'visit family' were just a cover. I'm not footing the bill for her and her lover's jaunts anymore," he said with a wry smile.

Lily closed the file and handed it back to him. He sat down on the bench beside her and said, "Lily, I needed this. I needed it to be over."

She nodded in understanding.

"I don't want this weighing on us anymore. We deserve the chance to figure out our future—together, without any secrets. When Pops showed me the papers in this first box, I realized I couldn't face all of this on my own. I need you by my side." He set the folder down on the bench and gently took Lily's hand. "Can we start fresh?"

"If you're sure that's what you really want."

His gaze locked on hers, caught off guard by her words.

"I mean..." She sighed, her breath catching slightly as she tried to find the right words. "I don't know what I mean." She ran a hand through her hair, trying to gather her scattered emotions. Then, she added, "Listen, let's not make any decisions until we figure out what the hell is going on, or at least what went on. We have no idea what else we'll find in those boxes. You might feel completely different once we're done."

He sat there for a moment, stunned. Her words stung more than he expected. His chest tightened as the weight of her response sank in. "Okay ... if that's what you want," he replied, his voice quieter, tinged with a mix of disappointment and resignation. He sat for a moment longer, his gaze dropping to the ground, then slowly stood up and began to walk inside.

As she watched him retreat, the hurt in his eyes tugged at her heart. Regretting the way her words had landed, she quickly called out, "Jet?"

He turned, his expression a mix of concern and vulnerability. The last thing she wanted was to hurt him, but she needed to give him a way out if he needed it. She had to protect him, absorb the blame if it came to that, and shield him from the burden of breaking her again. But she couldn't let him think she didn't want him. *Tell him!*

"Listen, my head is so messed up right now," she began, her voice trembling. "I love you. Always have, always will. That'll never change, but I'm scared. Because something—someone—always comes between us. I don't know how many more times I can lose you and still stay whole." Her voice cracked as tears welled in her eyes, blurring her vision as she watched him approach.

He knelt in front of her, gently cradling her face in his hands. His thumbs brushed away the stray tears that escaped. His gaze was steady, full of conviction, as he spoke, "Lil, you've never lost me."

"But I have, Jet. So many times. When I was too young and watched you with all those other girls ... when I was taken, and lost twenty years with you. Then, when I found out you were married, I thought I had lost you forever ... and now—God knows what else we'll find in those damn boxes. If something else takes you from me again—"

"Hey," he interrupted gently. "I've always loved *you*. *Never* anyone else! Nothing *ever* stopped our love, Lil. Time, distance, even this bloody sham of a marriage—nothing broke our bond. Do you hear me? I've always loved *you*. I'll say it a million more times until you believe me if I have to. I'm serious, no matter what comes out of this—no matter how bad or shocking it gets—my love for you will never change. It never has." His breath was warm against her face, his words grounding her as they sank in. "You're everything to me. I've never felt for anyone the way I feel for you. Come here."

With that, he pulled her close, his lips meeting hers in a tear-filled kiss that spoke volumes—of love, promise, and unyielding connection.

When the kiss ended, he kept his hands on her face, eyes searching hers for silent reassurance.

She nodded tearfully, feeling a sense of peace she hadn't felt in a long time. Just then, Ana stepped out onto the porch, her cheerful voice cutting through the moment.

"Dinner's ready!" Ana called, blissfully unaware of the emotional intensity in the air.

Jet gave Lily one last reassuring look before standing and offering her his hand to help her up. Together, they walked inside.

Chapter Fifteen

Fight or Flight

(2021)

Lilly was up well before dawn the following day. She put the kettle on and began going through her box of files. She arranged each file according to date and started at the beginning. Birth records, hers, and that of her parents.

Jet was right; Emil Daniel was related to her. He was her grandfather on her father's side. Her birth certificate confirmed Daria was born in Athens, Georgia, in 1984. The names on the document confirmed Joanna Lovell and Marik Daniels were her parents. The S must have been added to the end when they came to the US. Her mother evidently never married him. The only marriage certificate she found under her mother's name was with her stepfather, Robert Reynolds. *Ugh*, just the thought of him sickened her, but she needed to move on.

There was another file on her grandparents, Wallace and Gillie Lovell. And another on Abraham and Minnie Lovell, her great-uncle and aunt. Wallace and Abraham were brothers who also migrated from Romania with their parents as children. There was no information on Gillie or Minnie as to when or if they migrated from anywhere.

But what really caught her attention was her father's mother's name. Sebina Marin. *Could it be? Jesus!* Tears ran down her face. *Oh, dear God … that means Jet's mom is my grandmother? Did Mum know all along? Oh holy shit, that makes Jet my … half-uncle? I think I'm gonna be sick*—her stomach retched. She sat the file down and ran to the bathroom upstairs, waking Jet.

When she came out, he was standing outside his door, leaning against the frame with his hair disheveled and rubbing sleep from his eyes. The bathroom light caught on his jawline, highlighting the shadow of scruff that made him look effortlessly rugged. *Jesus … this man.*

Her gaze betrayed her as it traveled slowly downward, starting at the curve of his neck where his loose-fitting tank hung carelessly, exposing a glimpse of his collarbone. The intricate ink peeking out over his shoulders and covering his arms caught her attention next—a collection of rock 'n' roll tattoos, bold and chaotic yet strangely beautiful. Snakes coiled around microphones, skulls intertwined with roses, and fragments of lyrics etched in cursive danced across his skin, telling a story of rebellion and raw emotion. Her eyes traced the colorful story as it wrapped around his toned biceps, down to the veins running along his forearms, before finally landing on his silk boxers. *Oh, lord.* The sight of his very obvious morning hard-on made her throat tighten, her breath hitching slightly.

"Hey, Lil," he murmured, his voice still thick with sleep, sending a shiver down her entire body. He shifted his stance, tilting his head to study her. "You okay? You coming down with something?"

The concern in his tone made her cheeks burn, snapping her out of her shameless ogling. "What?" she stammered, dragging her eyes back up to his face. "No. No, I'm fine. Just—must've been something I ate."

His lips curled into a small, knowing smile. "Uh, huh?" He crossed his arms over his chest, the movement drawing her attention to the way the tank clung to his torso. "You sure you're not feverish?"

Her mouth opened to respond, but no words came out. How the hell was she supposed to form coherent sentences when he looked like that?

"Uh, no ... sorry, I'm fine now." She glanced downward again. *STOOOOOP it. look up, look up!!* He caught her this time, and she couldn't help but give him a sly smile. "I'll just ... be downstairs." She did her best not to look down again as she made her way past him.

His eyes sparkling with mischief as he grinned, pleased that he caught her looking. Then, seizing the moment and hoping she would respond favorably, he grabbed her by the waist and pulled her toward him, pressing her body tight against his. With his arms securely around her, he leaned in, tilting his head as he went in for a kiss.

But she turned away, covering her mouth as he missed and got her cheek.

"Sorry, my breath."

She quickly scooted away from him, blushing because she got caught, and headed back downstairs. Jet scratched his head and walked into the bathroom.

When she returned to the kitchen, determined to banish the lingering image of those silk boxers, she pulled her birth files together and stacked them back into the box. A faint scent of aging paper tickled her nose as she reached for the file on Marik.

Opening the file, she ran her fingers over the pages as she immersed herself in the details. According to the records, Marik was born in 1968 to Emil Daniel and Sebina Marin.

Still struggling to come to terms with the shocking revelation of what she had read earlier, she could only imagine how Pops must feel. She had hidden a whole other life before she met him. He didn't know her at all, did he? And evidently, neither did she. *How do I even wrap my head around her being my grandmother? Is this why she had her brother take me? So I wouldn't marry my uncle? Well, half Uncle. Does that make it better somehow? Is this what's going to take him from me, once and for all!! FUCK! This is worse than FUCK ... what's worse than Fuck?!!! ... Double Fuck!!*

She closed the file, plopped her elbows on the table, and massaged her temples, squeezing her eyes closed. *Breathe, dammit.* She took a deep breath and blew it out slowly.

Do I tell him or do I wait? Hide the box! Yeah, hide the damn box ... make it the last one we look at. That way, I save the worst for last ... Jesus, what if this isn't the worst ... UGH, I can't do this right now!

She slammed the file back in the box, but as she put it back in its place, another file with her stepfather's name on it caught her attention. Only two items were in the file, both newspaper clippings.

Deadly Shootout on 78th Avenue Leaves Two Dead, Community Reeling

March 19, 2000

A normally quiet neighborhood on 78th Avenue North was rocked by gunfire on the evening of March 17th, leaving two people dead and one injured in a violent confrontation with police.

The incident began at approximately 6:30 pm when neighbors reported a heated argument outside 736 78th Ave North. Police arrived at the scene shortly thereafter, only for the situation to escalate dramatically.

According to witnesses, Robert and Joanna Reynolds, the couple renting the property, emerged from the home brandishing firearms. Police, perceiving an imminent threat, returned fire, fatally wounding both individuals. Another person at the scene was injured during the exchange but is expected to recover.

Authorities have not confirmed whether the Reynolds fired at officers, and an investigation is underway to determine the sequence of events leading to the tragic standoff.

A subsequent search of the property uncovered a cache of firearms, a significant amount of cash, and various amounts of illegal drugs and paraphernalia. Several other individuals present at the residence were taken into custody in connection with the incident.

The shocking events have left neighbors stunned, with many expressing disbelief over the level of violence. "This is a safe neighborhood. We've never seen anything like this before," one resident said.

As police continue their investigation, the community mourns the loss of life and grapples with the disturbing revelations surrounding the incident.

Obituary: Joanna Lovell-Reynolds (1968 - 2000)

It is with deep sorrow and heavy hearts that we announce the untimely passing of Joanna Lovell-Reynolds, born on February 12, 1968, to Wallace and Gillie Lovell. Joanna passed away on March 17, 2000, in a tragic incident at the age of 32.

Joanna leaves behind her daughter, Daria Daniels, born in 1984. She is also survived by her parents, Wallace and Gillie Lovell, whose hearts are broken at the loss of their daughter.

Although Joanna's life was cut short far too soon, her memory will live on in the hearts of her family, friends, and all who were fortunate enough to know her.

A memorial service will be held to honor Joanna's life. Details will be shared with friends and family. In lieu of flowers, we kindly ask for your thoughts and prayers during this time.

Lily covered her mouth and squeezed her eyes shut, holding back a shrieking gasp. Her throat tightened and burned, and her chest felt like a thousand knives were stabbing her all at once as every heartbeat sent waves of pain coursing through her body. *Nooo!! Mama!?* She couldn't breathe, and she couldn't scream.

All she could do was let the floodgates open up as she dropped the clippings. They fell to the floor as she left the kitchen and headed for the front door. She needed to go; she couldn't fall apart right there in Pops' kitchen.

Grabbing her keys and a jacket, she got into the Beast and started her up. The engine roared. Jet knew precisely what he was hearing. He had taken a shower and was getting dressed when Pops came out of his room and asked, "Was that the Beast? Where is she going at this hour?"

Jet hurriedly descended the stairs, fumbling to put on his shirt as he reached the door, only to catch a glimpse of her speeding away down the street. Concern filled him as he too wondered where she drove off to.

The kitchen light was left on and as he entered, he noticed Lily must've been working on some of the files. He went to take the box off the table and saw the articles on the floor. He picked them up and read them. "Shit," he said under his breath.

Pops walked in about that time and saw Jet's expression. "What's the matter, son?" Jet showed him the clippings. Seeing the look on his father's face, Jet realized he had seen the articles before. Pops sat down at the table and sighed. Jet could see the pain in his eyes.

Realizing that his father had been just as much a victim in this charade as he and Lily, he couldn't be mad at him.

"Was this one of the boxes you went through too?" Pops nodded. "You forgot to mention Lily's mom was involved."

"What would have been the point, son? You asked about her father being involved. He wasn't. I just left it at that. After everything you two had been through, I didn't think adding that would help matters."

"Yeah, you're probably right." He slumped in his chair.

They sat silently for a moment, then heard Ana enter through the front door. She joined them in the kitchen and found both men sitting with blank stares. "Have you had your breakfast yet?" she asked.

Pops didn't answer, so Jet did. "No, Ana, he hasn't. Since you are here now, I need to run out for a while." He stood to make his exit.

Pops grabbed Jet's arm as he passed and said, "Go find her son. She must be beside herself right now."

Jet put his hand on Pop's shoulder and gave him a quick squeeze and a reassuring look.

Now realizing she must've walked in on a family matter, Ana said, "Are you looking for Miss Lily?"

"Yes," Jet said.

"I saw the monster down at the park when I passed."

Jet and Pops both smiled and corrected her. "The Beast."

"Oh, yes, the Beast."

"Thanks, Ana." Jet kissed her on the cheek as he headed out. "I'm taking your car, Pops."

"Yeah, yeah." Pops waved him off.

Jet drove to the park and pulled up next to the Beast. He sat looking through the windshield, scanning the area for any sign of her. He remembered her favorite hiding spot, the troll bridge.

As he walked towards her, he couldn't help but notice the recent addition of two benches on either side of the small bridge, which was now much too small for her to hide under. She was sitting, legs crossed, one over the other, wiping tears from her eyes. When she saw him approaching, she quickly tried to compose herself.

He had no idea what to say, so he remained silent, sitting down beside her on the bench. Gently, he wrapped his arm around her, feeling the settling comfort of her body against his. She nestled herself into the curve of his arm, resting her head on his shoulder. Together, they sat in the darkness, accompanied only by the soft glow of the streetlamps that trickled down the park's winding path.

Finally, she spoke. "When you were a kid, before you met me, did you ever think your life would turn out like this? I mean, If I hadn't shown up and blown your world all to hell?"

"Lily, you didn't blow anything to hell; our parents did. I'm sorry about your mom. I didn't know. And Pops didn't say anything because, when he told me about your stepfather, he didn't think it was pertinent to our conversation. I saw the clippings on the floor this morning. I wish you had said something."

"I think I was in shock more than anything. Also, I think that, in the back of my mind, I always figured Rob would get her killed one day. Even though I haven't had any contact or seen her in years, I just always thought she was there, ya know, in case I wanted to." She broke down in tears again.

He squeezed her tightly as she tried to calm herself and continue. "But that's not the only reason I needed to get out of there. Did you mean it when you said you didn't care how bad the news was? That we would get through it."

His voice was firm as he spoke to her, pulling her chin up to meet his gaze. "Yes. I told you I'm not going anywhere, and you better not go anywhere either," he said, emphasizing each word. "I mean it. Lil, we're meant to be together. All the shit, and all the heartache, and all the lies ... and we still fall into each other's path. It's proof. It's *my* proof, anyway. So, no more hiding or holding back, and no more running from me when you're angry or upset."

He let go of her chin as she looked out at the park, her thoughts racing. Jet spoke again, this time more softly, "We're in this together, Lil, and I'm not letting you out of my sight anymore ... you hear me?" He spoke with determination and a commitment to their relationship.

She nodded, becoming emotional once more. She pulled Jet's hand around her shoulder and held it to her cheek. "Hey, look at me." She obeyed as he leaned in and kissed her, slowly and softly, then sat back, watching her face, knowing she had more to say.

"Okay..." She took a deep breath, looking back out over the park, and explained, "So, it's not just my mom, Jet. I couldn't sleep, so I went through my box this morning. I pulled some of my files out to read through, and you were right; Emil and I are related. I wasn't sure when or how to tell you this, but ..." She sat up straight and turned to face him, bringing her knee between them. "He's my grandfather on my father's side."

He looked surprised but not shocked. "Okay." He nodded. "So, we have another clue, good. This is good. We're getting somewhere."

Ignoring his comment, she swallowed hard and blurted, "My grandmother's name, Emil's wife, was Sebina Marin."

His eyes grew wide. "My Mum, Sebina? Wait, that would mean..."

She finished his sentence. "That my biological father, Marik, and you are half-brothers, making you my half-uncle."

"Lily, that's crazy! No way!?"

She shrugged. "I don't have all the details, only what I put together from the files."

"You must have read them wrong."

She shook her head. "Pretty sure I didn't, but you can look at them when we get back."

He dropped his head, stretched his neck from side to side, popping it, and said, "Jesus, Lil, how much more can we take?"

Trying to lighten the mood, she shrugged. "Hmm, not sure, Uncle John."

He looked at her sharply, then grinned. "Fuck You." That made her laugh out loud. Then he said, "Seriously, though."

"Well, I mean, honestly, the worst part is already over, as far as that's concerned."

"What do you mean?"

"We've already had a child together, and he's grown. If there were any genetic issues, we would've caught them by now. Soo…"

"Thank God for that, at least."

"I just don't understand how she could have allowed us to date if she knew all this. Ya know?"

"Yeah, I just thought about that too, and why the kidnapping? If her issue was that we were related, why did she have to take you so far away and hide you from us? Why not just tell us?"

"Maybe because she didn't want your dad to know about her past?"

"Possibly, but I still think we're missing something."

She sighed. "Yeah." She turned her back to rest on the bench as he pulled her closer and wrapped his arm around her again.

They sat quietly, lost in thought, contemplating their latest discoveries as they stared out at the horizon. The darkness of the night gradually gave way to the sunrise, and after a few more moments of contemplation, Jet broke the silence and suggested they head out to grab some breakfast.

Chapter Sixteen

Under the Willow

(2021)

They drove to a little café Jet liked on the outskirts of town for breakfast near one of his favorite golf clubs. They took the Beast, leaving Pop's car at the park. Jet drove, thinking a long drive and some food would help their moods.

Having a full stomach and a calmer mind, Lily offered to drive the Beast back to the park so he could pick up Pop's car. She took a detour through some country roads and turned onto a dirt road that likely led to a farmhouse. Passing some fencing, she noticed a large willow tree with a heavy canopy hanging low, and she pulled the Beast under it.

"What are we doing here?"

She put the Beast in park and turned the engine off. Ignoring his query, she pushed her seat back, climbed onto his lap, and faced him.

"Babe, what are you doing?" Jet's voice was a mix of curiosity and caution as he scanned the surroundings, the mid-morning sun casting flickering shadows of willow leaves through the car. A half-laugh escaped him as he turned his attention back to her. "Lily, hey, uh … as much as I am enjoying your intention, we may want to find a more private spot."

Still ignoring him, her fingers dove into his curls, clutching them tight, and holding him still as she plunged her tongue into his mouth, claiming ownership of *him* this time.

The taste of her—familiar and intoxicating. *Fuck it*, he thought, his hands sliding under her T-shirt. *No bra?* The realization hit him like a lightning bolt, shooting a throbbing ache into his already tight jeans. *How did I miss this?*

Lily had grabbed Jet's jacket as she left the house this morning. It was the only one hanging by the door as she left. It hung loosely, covering her entire body except for about an inch of hem at the bottom of her skirt. Now she was yanking it off, the stiff fabric sliding off her shoulders. Jet's breath hitched as his eyes roamed over her, memories flooding back to a time when sneaking away in his car was their only escape from the crowded flat.

Lily leaned in close, her mischievous grin faltering as her fingers gripped the edge of Jet's shirt. "Shhhhhh …" she breathed, her lips brushing his ear. Her hands slipped under the fabric, warmth meeting warmth as she tugged the shirt free from his jeans.

With determined fingers, she unfastened the buttons, her heart beating a wild rhythm against her ribs. The shirt fell away, revealing his chest in the soft light.

Her breath caught in her throat as her gaze froze on the large tattoo covering his heart—a broken butterfly, its wings fractured, inked with such delicate lines that they seemed to shudder with every breath he took. The jagged edges of the wings reaching skyward. This tattoo wasn't just ink; it was a scar, a silent reminder of the torment he'd endured while she was gone.

"Jet …" she whispered, almost a gasp. His name hung on her lips. Her fingers hovered just above the ink, afraid to touch, as if the butterfly might crumble with the slightest breeze.

Her hand finally found the courage to move, the tips of her fingers tracing the torn and shattered wings with a tenderness that made Jet's breath catch. The world around them—the rustle of the willow's branches, the distant hum of insects—faded into silence.

Her voice was barely more than a whisper. "It's beautiful." Then, a visceral realization hit her like a punch to the chest, leaving her breathless. "This is because of me, isn't it?"

Jet's jaw tightened as he swallowed hard, feeling as though another dark secret had just been revealed. "I needed you close," he admitted, his voice a low rasp, heavy with years of repressed grief. "I needed something—anything—to remind me that there was still light in the world. That there was still you."

Jet's thoughts spun, the weight of her touch and her tears crashing into him like waves. He had waited for this—for her—not just the physical closeness, but the understanding, the shared pain she had not fully realized until now. Seeing her like this—vulnerable and guilt-ridden—it was like a dam breaking.

He couldn't stop staring at her, the way her hands trembled as she touched him, as if she were afraid she might break him further. But it wasn't validation or resentment he felt—it was relief. Finally, she was in the same head space with him. They were no longer running from the ghosts of their past.

She thinks she broke me. His chest tightening as he held onto her. *She doesn't see it. She doesn't know that the only thing that kept me alive all these years was the memory of her, the hope that someday she'd come back.*

God, she's everything. The thought hit him with startling clarity. Even in her brokenness, even through the pain she'd caused, she was still the only one who could make him feel whole.

As her hands moved over him, the need to protect her, to comfort her, to claim her all at once swelled inside him. He wanted to tell her it was okay, that they didn't have to rush this—that just being here, together, was enough. But the look in her eyes stopped him.

It wasn't just guilt or sorrow that he saw. It was need. For him. For this moment. For them. And he wasn't about to deny her—or himself—any longer.

Her hand stilled over his heart, the warmth of his skin beneath her palm anchoring her. "I did this to you." she murmured, her voice barely audible. "I've been so selfish in my grief. I foolishly believed you were okay, somehow. I know you said you weren't ... but you were free. You were here, at home with your family, and the boys ... I thought you at least had people." She sounded almost confused.

Jet caught her hand in his, pressing her palm firmly against the tattoo. His touch was steady, but his eyes betrayed a hurricane of emotions—anger, sorrow, forgiveness. "But, I didn't have you ... you're here now," he said, his voice rough but resolute. "I told you, that's all that matters. We're here."

More tears spilled over, carving silent paths down her cheeks. She shook her head, biting her lip against the sob rising in her chest. "Is it enough?" she choked out. "Is it enough for everything I took from you?"

She pulled back slightly, her gaze meeting his. In his eyes, she saw not judgment but the unwavering patience and love she knew would be there. It was too much—too raw, too overwhelming.

"You didn't take anything. They did, remember."

"But *you* didn't know that. All those years you thought I left you. That I didn't love you." Her eyes fixed on the shattered edges of his beautiful broken butterfly. Her fractured butterfly. "I'm so sorry ... I can't stand that you thought I had given up on us ..."

When her lips crashed into his, he felt the last of his restraint crumble. Every unspoken word, every sleepless night, every ache he had buried deep down surged to the surface.

"Don't run from it," he breathed, his voice steady and unyielding. "Feel it, Lil. Feel it with me."

For a moment, she hesitated, a war waging in her chest between the guilt and need that tangled inside her. Her body screamed for him, for a way to escape this heavy burden, her heart still mired in the sorrow of the scars she'd left on him.

Her breath came in shallow bursts as she looked down at him, trying to make sense of the turmoil inside. "I'm sorry, I don't know what to do, how to fix this. How to fix you ... I'm the one who always needed fixing," she whispered, her voice a fragile thread.

His voice was low, a calm amidst her storm. "It's okay. I'm okay ... we're okay, in this moment—that's all we can control right now."

She was quiet now. Her eyes switched their gaze from the fractured butterfly to his concerned eyes.

Jet studied her for a long moment, his jaw tightening. He knew her well enough to recognize her retreat, to see the way she was closing herself off even as she reached for him. But he couldn't deny her—not when she was hurting, not if this was the only way she felt she could release the turmoil raging inside her, even if he knew it wasn't really what she needed.

He relented. His hands grabbed her hips, drawing her closer. The act became a silent promise, a bittersweet collision of need and love, of pain and release.

She pulled her tee shirt over her head; the fabric sliding off her skin as if shedding not only the shirt but the weight of everything she'd been carrying. Ebbing the storm inside her as their bodies moved together, her guilt and grief momentarily giving way to the mercy only he could offer.

Jet's hands moved to her breasts, his touch tender and electrifying. His thumbs brushed over the sensitive peaks, sending waves through her, causing her flesh to tighten in response to his touch.

Her skin was soft and smoldering, each touch stirring an unspoken invitation—every sensation heightened as he pulled her closer, his lips seeking the heat of her body.

Her hands weren't idle. With one hand gripping the seat back for support, Lily deftly undid his pants, the sound of the buckle releasing mingling with their heavy, synchronized breathing. His erection sprang free, and she eagerly tugged her panties aside, positioning herself above him.

The slow, tantalizing descent onto his shaft sent waves of pleasure coursing through both of them, their shared gasp of satisfaction filling the small space.

A stillness hung in the air as their bodies tuned perfectly to one another. She clenched around him. A surge of raw desire passed between them. The sensation of her tightening sent a shock through his system. His breath snarled, a low groan escaping his lips as he thrust into her.

But she trapped him with her weight, grinding him to a halt. The determination in her eyes was palpable, her need to take control clear. *Jesus … this girl is on a mission.* Yielding, he relaxed his hold, surrendering to her as she began to move, the rhythm of her hips driving him to the edge of madness.

Sliding down in the seat a little to give her more room, Jet watched in awe as she rode him, her movements fluid and confident. The sight of her—the woman he loved, the woman who was driving him wild—was almost too much to bear.

His hands roamed her body, caressing her thighs, gripping her ass, and again finding their way to her breasts. The feel of her under his touch, the way she arched back in response, her breath erratic and shallow, almost matching his own, sent him spiraling closer to the edge.

Her hair fell around them like a curtain, her scent enveloping him as she leaned in to kiss him. The longer she rode him, the faster her pace, the more frenzied he became. He was close—so close—and didn't want it to end just yet. With a sudden surge of strength, Jet took over, grabbing her and holding her tight against him, stopping her frantic movements.

She gave in silently this time, her breath mingling with his as they both took a moment to recover. Then, with a deep, unhurried intensity, he began to move again, his thrusts slow and deliberate, each one driving them both closer to the brink.

The air around them was thick with the scent of their passion, a heady mix of sweat, earth, and desire. The sound of their breaths, their moans, filled the space, creating a rhythm all their own. As Jet reached the peak of pleasure, his body tensed, his shaft pulsing inside her, sending shockwaves through them both.

Lily tightened around him, her release crashing over her, leaving her breathless. For a moment, the world was silent, their bodies and hearts beating as one in a fragile, shared rhythm. Slowly, reality seeped back in, and she let out a long, shaky sigh, dropping her head back, exhaustion and relief washing over her in equal measure.

She moved carefully, her fingers brushing his chest one last time before she leaned over to grab her T-shirt from the driver's seat. She pulled it over her head with a deliberate slowness, her hands lingering for a moment as if grounding herself. Her eyes remained fixed ahead, her thoughts a tangled storm.

Jet watched her intently, searching her face for any sign of what she was feeling. He expected a smile, a word—something—but the silence between them stretched, heavy and uncertain.

She shifted off him, her movements hesitant, almost reluctant, and adjusted her clothing. Still, she didn't speak.

The quiet gnawed at him until he finally broke it. "Lil, are we okay?" His voice was soft, tentative.

She paused, her fingers tightening around the keys in the ignition. For a heartbeat, she didn't answer. Then, as the Beast rumbled to life, she murmured, "Therapy."

The word seemed to hang in the air. Jet tilted his head, his brows furrowing. "Therapy?" he echoed, his tone a mix of amusement and concern.

Lily shifted in her seat, staring out the windshield, her hands gripping the wheel and the gearshift as though it were the only thing tethering her to the moment. Her voice was quiet but steady when she finally spoke again. "It's not enough ... it will probably never be enough ... feeling you again. Reminding myself I'm actually here. That *we're* here."

The vulnerability in her words hit Jet sharp and unexpected, leaving him reeling. Reaching out, he placed his hand over hers, his grip firm but gentle. "You don't have to do this alone," he said, his voice thick with emotion. "Ever again."

She turned her head slightly, her eyes shimmering with unspoken sorrow and gratitude. "I know. But sometimes ... it's the only way I know how."

Jet's hand tightened around hers. "You don't have to fight so hard, Lil. Not with me. Not anymore."

Her lips quirked into a faint, fleeting smile as she looked back to the road, shifting the Beast into gear. "Maybe I need to remind myself of that, too."

He let out a small laugh, low and warm, trying to lighten the mood just enough to ease the weight between them. "Well, if that was therapy, we're gonna need multiple weekly sessions. You know, for health purposes."

The corners of her mouth twitched, her voice carrying a hint of teasing. "I guess that makes you certified, huh?"

Jet grinned, his crooked smile breaking through the lingering tension. "Or certifiable … either way, I'll be sure to bill you later."

Lily shook her head as they turned onto the blacktop. Her smile softened, this time reaching her eyes. For the first time in a long time, she felt a flicker of peace—fragile but real.

Chapter Seventeen

It's Gotta Be Tonight

(2021)

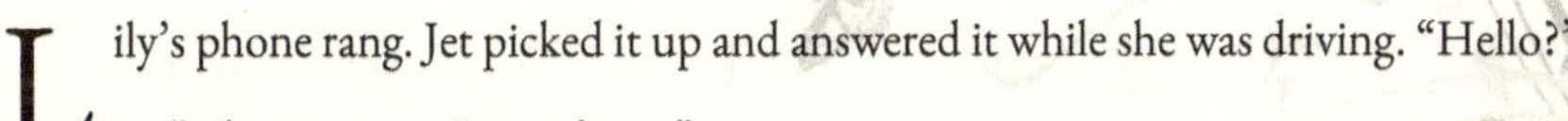

Lily's phone rang. Jet picked it up and answered it while she was driving. "Hello?"

"Uh, is my ... is Daria there?"

"May I ask who's calling?"

"Her son, Jack." Jet sat silent for a moment. When Lily looked over at him, he grimaced.

She pulled off into a car park and took the phone from him. "Hello?"

"Mom?"

"Hey, baby, are you okay? It's so early there?"

"Yeah, umm, so I just got a call from the doctor."

"Uncle's doctor?" She looked over at Jet and switched to the speaker.

"Yeah, she wanted to know if you were still in the States."

"What did you tell her?"

"I told her you had gone home to see your family. Was that okay?"

"Uh ... yeah, that's fine."

"I figured it was them that sent all of our stuff to us. They had to expect you would leave, right?"

"One would think."

"She gave me a number to call her if I spoke to you. She said it was urgent, but I didn't want to give her your direct number until I spoke to you."

"You did good, Hun. Did she say what was so urgent?"

"No, just that it was imperative that she get in touch with you as soon as possible."

"Okay, text me the number when we hang up."

"Mom, what's going on?"

"I have no idea, Hun. I'll let you know as soon as I find something out."

"Okay."

"Don't worry, Jack. I'm sure it's just something to do with Uncle's estate or something like that."

"Okay, I'll let you deal with her ... Hey, who was that who answered the phone? Was it him? Was that John?"

Lily looked over at Jet. "Yes, baby. It was."

"I thought you weren't looking for him anymore since he was married."

"Well, actually, he sort of found *me*, but it's a long story. Let me find out what's going on with the doctor, and I'll call you back and tell you the whole thing."

"Okay, Mom, I love you. Be safe, and I'll talk to you later."

"Okay, baby, love you too! Bye now."

A couple of seconds passed, and she heard the alert on her phone. Ding. Ding. She took a deep breath and tapped the screen to see the number.

"Who's the doctor?" Jet asked.

"She would be the one who Andrei brought in for our healthcare. Another Romanian."

"Hmm, what do you want to do?"

"Let's get to the house first. I want to see something before I call her."

They picked up Pop's car and drove to the house. As soon as they walked in, Lily headed straight for the boxes in the kitchen. She pulled out the pictures from the first box.

"These are the pictures I pulled of the people I recognized, remember?" She rifled through the pile until she found what she was looking for. "Do you know this person?"

"Yeah, that's my Aunt Lavina, Uncle Andrei's wife."

"Fuck!" Shaking her head, she put the picture down, got her phone out, and opened her text messages.

"Why, who is she to you?"

"The doctor," she said as she tapped the call icon on her phone.

"Hello?"

"Lavina, this is Daria. Jack said you called looking for me?"

"Yes, I take it you are with John since you know my real name."

"Yes, what's going on?"

"I wanted to warn you of a potential situation."

She put the call on speaker so Jet could hear. "What situation?"

"We sent Frank and Sebina some boxes of information on the family at the same time we sent you your information on Jack's eighteenth birthday. Have you had the opportunity to go through them yet?"

"Not all, but some. Why?"

"I am returning to the States to get Jack and his wife. Please arrange a safe place for them to stay."

"Lavina! Tell me what's going on! Safe from what?"

"How much have you read about Marik?"

"Just the basics. I know he's my biological father and Jet's half-brother."

"Well, it seems he mobilized a coup d'état after Emil passed," Lavina added.

"Wait, what do you mean?"

"I will explain everything when I see you. Do you have a safe place to house Jack or not?"

She looked at Jet, and he nodded and said, "They can stay at the estate with us. It's secluded, and there's plenty of room." He looked at Lily to try and convince her, then said, "When I upgraded the pub, I also upgraded the compound's security."

"Good, John. I will send a team to help with surveillance. Daria, do you have your pack with you?"

"No, you can't bring that stuff on commercial planes. Honestly, I didn't think I was going to need it."

"Daria, what have I told you, time and time again?" Lavina chastised her.

"Oh, for Christ's sake, seriously."

"Say it!"

"Never let your guard down!"

"Good. Now, there is a box labeled Trusa. It should have everything you need in it. Please find it and take Frank and Ana to the compound. I'll send her instructions momentarily."

Jet asked, "Ana?"

Lily raised one eyebrow and shook her head, then closed her eyes in exasperation. "Of course, she works with you!" Lily ground her teeth, then continued sarcastically, "Make sure to tell her to bring her pack!"

"Ana is always prepared."

Lily rolled her eyes.

"Okay." Ignoring the sarcasm in Lavina's voice, she asked. "Can you give me an ETA?"

"We will be landing within the hour. Tell Jack to have his pack ready. We will not be traveling commercially."

"Got it." Lily hung up and shook her head in disbelief, then said, "She knew I was here the whole time!"

"What?"

"You think Ana didn't report my being here the second I showed up?"

"Oh ... but I hired her from an agency?"

Lily rolled her eyes and gave him a look like, C'mon, Jet, catch up! Then she called Jack.

He answered, "Hey, Baby, it's go time. Pack it up and bring your kit. The doctor will be there in an hour or so. By the way, her name is Lavina, and she is your actual aunt."

"Yeah, uh, I already knew that. About Lavina, that is."

"We're gonna have a serious talk when you get here!"

"Love you, Mom!" he said super-fast with a half laugh and hung up.

Lily told Jet to bring the rest of the boxes down while she gathered up the ones from the kitchen. There were five boxes altogether. When Jet finished, Lily found the box labeled Trusa. She set it on the kitchen table and went upstairs to pack her bag and change.

When she came down, she pulled everything out as Ana and Frank entered the room. She gave Ana a weary, side-eyed look and said, "Nice to finally meet you, Ana, or do we call you something else?"

With zero emotion, Ana replied, "Ana will do."

Lily nodded, then strapped on a leg holster carrying an M9-22. Then she pulled on a shoulder holster, checked the magazine, and placed a Beretta 92X RDO into the sheath. She tried to hand Jet a 3032 Tomcat, but he refused to take it.

Holding his hands up, he said, "What the hell, Lil, are we going to war?" Shaking his head. "I've never shot a gun in my life; hell, I've never even touched one."

"You're getting ready to get a crash course, Babe." Giving him a determined look.

When he continued to refuse the pistol, she placed it in her back waistband and threw on her leather jacket. She counted the magazines, put an extra for each weapon in her jacket pockets, gathered what was left, and placed it all in her duffle bag.

She looked at Ana and said, "We ready?" Ana nodded. "We're taking the Beast and all the boxes. Maybe we can learn more while waiting for the kids."

They grabbed the boxes and headed out. When they got to Jet's estate, he showed everyone where they would be staying. Frank, Ana, and the kids would stay in the main house with Lily and Jet. Ronny and Reggie had headed home for a few weeks. Jet figured the security team and whoever else showed up would stay in the extra wing next to the studio.

Lily and Jet got everyone settled before unloading the boxes into the studio. Together, they began sorting through the files as quickly as possible. When Lily came across a set of documents that resembled a journal written by Andrei, she sat down on the couch to read them.

Chapter Eighteen

Yester-days

(1953 - 1978)

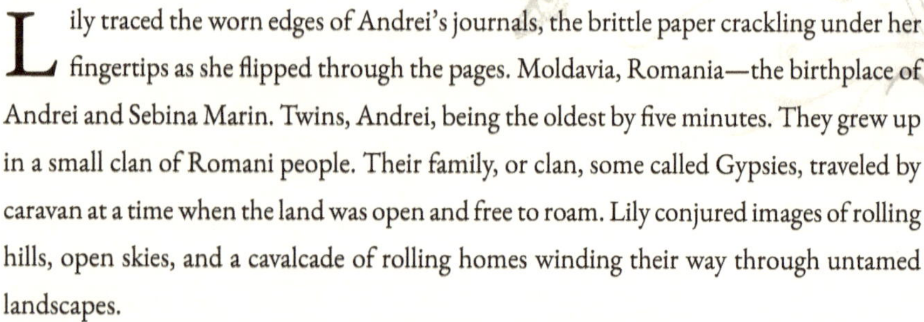

Lily traced the worn edges of Andrei's journals, the brittle paper crackling under her fingertips as she flipped through the pages. Moldavia, Romania—the birthplace of Andrei and Sebina Marin. Twins, Andrei, being the oldest by five minutes. They grew up in a small clan of Romani people. Their family, or clan, some called Gypsies, traveled by caravan at a time when the land was open and free to roam. Lily conjured images of rolling hills, open skies, and a cavalcade of rolling homes winding their way through untamed landscapes.

Her heart quickened as she pieced together their story before Sebina's arrival in Leeds. Bound by more than blood, they had grown up in a world where survival demanded cunning, and Andrei's descriptions of their childhood painted a stark picture. Although their father, Stephan, worked alongside their uncle, selling copper vessels and carafes, Andrei wrote that the life of a Roma child was not one of innocence but of necessity: children scavenged, begging, and stealing—anything to help make ends meet.

Despite these cultural hardships, Andrei and Sebina's family was not destitute. They weren't rich by any means, but they were skilled and well-respected within their community. Stephan's craftsmanship, particularly his intricate copper pieces, was admired and sought after. Their uncle's business acumen ensured they were never entirely without opportunities. The family was known for its resourcefulness, loyalty to one another, and deep-rooted traditions, which it upheld with pride even in the face of adversity.

Although times had changed since then, growing up Roma in any era meant growing up quickly and learning to take care of yourself. Andrei's journal revealed that his and Sebina's childhood was no exception.

It would be an understatement to say that the two were close. Andrei loved and cared for his sister, sharing with her the best of the spoils they had gathered at the end of each day. Similarly, Sebina adored and admired her older brother, who acted as her protector and partner in crime. They spent their days together, scheming and devising new ways to swindle and pilfer from the locals.

Andrei had an entrepreneurial spirit from a young age, quickly learning how to identify the needs of others and fulfilling those needs at a price. This skill evidently proved valuable later in life.

At the young age of ten, he had already formed a group of children of different ages to spy on locals. They would report back to Andrei, and he would use the information to devise schemes.

Sebina, the ever-willing decoy, would engage the target, either luring them away or distracting them. Lily could almost see the two of them, Sebina's bright eyes scanning a market while Andrei lingered in the shadows, calculating his next move and putting his team to work.

As the mastermind behind his small enterprise, Andrei realized he needed more than his wits to succeed. He recruited older men to act as his muscle, which helped him maintain his influence and authority amongst his crew.

Andrei compensated them reasonably well, not always in cash, but also through favors. He was surprised how a small favor could make a significant impact on preserving loyalty and earning respect within his community.

Little did he know that, just two short years later, his particular set of skills would come into play. Sebina's abduction at twelve was described with chilling detail.

Lily's chest tightened as she read about the men from another clan who had taken her. Forcing her into marriage, as was customary in some traveling clans of the time. Andrei's despair manifested on the ink-stained pages, his single-minded determination to find his sister leaping out at her.

According to the journal, twenty-two-year-old Emil Daniel wasn't just a horse trader's son. Andrei had often heard the elders speak in hushed tones about him. He was infamous in their world—envy and ambition burned through his veins, especially when it came to Alexei Boswell, the so-called King of the Gypsies. So, when Emil appeared in the same village as the Marin clan, Andrei knew trouble was near. What he didn't realize was how close that trouble would strike.

Andrei had stepped into a shop to buy his little sister a sweet, leaving her humming happily on a stone barrier outside. It was supposed to be a simple, safe moment. But by the time he came back, Sebina was gone. The bustling street—full of carts, animals, and people going about their day—offered no answers. She had disappeared as if swallowed by the chaos.

Andrei had written about the panic, the crushing fear, when he realized she wasn't anywhere to be found. He described returning to the camp, breathless and frantic, and seeing his family's faces crumble as he told them what had happened. Lily could feel the raw guilt behind his words, even as he detailed how the entire camp mobilized, searching through the night to find her.

The truth, though, came later—bits and pieces gathered from whispers in market stalls or casual comments from other clans during their travels. Emil had taken Sebina, forcing her into a marriage to claw his way back into the Boswell family's favor.

He wrote about the years, three to be exact, he spent searching for her, scouring every town and village they passed through, chasing every lead, calling in every favor. He described the endless roads, the sleepless nights, and the hollow ache that came with every dead end.

Andrei's anguish was unmistakable. It wasn't just about bringing his sister home—it was about undoing the failure he felt in that moment he'd left her alone. An emotion that Jet had expressed about his own perceived failures—his voice echoed in her memory, rough and broken, as he confessed to carrying that weight, too. The shared thread of guilt and love bound Andrei's and Jet's past in a way that left her breathless. Then, remembering Andrei's comment about her and Jack being his most precious assets, finally made sense.

It was sheer luck that the two clans crossed paths near a copper village when stopping for supplies for his father and uncle. Andrei had finally found Sebina. One day, while putting his crew to work looking for the perfect marks in this new town, he immediately recognized the now fifteen-year-old Sebina. She and another girl her age had come to the town market to buy cloth.

He waited for her to be alone at a merchant's table, approaching her from behind while pretending to inspect the peddlers' wares. Andrei whispered to her not to speak or look at him while he gave her instructions to walk back to her caravan so he could find her later. Then, he set in motion a plan for her escape. Sebina, following her brother's instructions, bought her cloth and returned to her tiny roving home.

When evening came, the men from her new clan sang, drank, and danced around the fire. Sebina stayed in the caravan. Eventually, when they all fell asleep on the ground outside, Andrei was able to sneak into the caravan and speak to Sebina. Not to his complete surprise, he found Sebina rocking her baby boy.

As the years passed, Andrei understood that his sister was highly likely to have children from this marriage. However, the situation was now more complicated because the child was male.

During this era, traditional Roma culture placed significant emphasis on male children, as they were expected to become the breadwinners and carry on the family name. Male children were typically taught the family trade and groomed to take on leadership roles within the clan. They were more likely to receive formal education and were entrusted with adult responsibilities at a younger age compared to their female counterparts.

While females are not less loved, their value is often seen differently in the eyes of tradition. In some families, it is not unheard of for girls to be promised in marriage as young as nine, exchanged to strengthen ties between clans. As with all clans, the women bear the weight of household duties—cooking, cleaning, and raising children—expectations passed down through generations. These roles, though cherished and vital to the family's survival, often place the future of a woman in the hands of those who claim her, rather than allowing her the chance to choose her own path.

So, in hushed voices, they argued. She pleaded with him to allow her to take the child with them, but he understood the dangers and refused. Sebina did not want to leave her son behind. He asked her point blank one last time if she wished to remain in the marriage. She answered no. Then, as her child became restless, and she turned to check on him, Andrei slipped behind her, wrapping an arm around her neck and pressing his bicep tight against her carotid artery. Within seconds, Sebina's struggling ceased, and she slumped unconscious.

The pages seemed to pulse with Andrei's anguish as he recounted his decision. To steal Sebina back was one thing, but to take her son? It would mean war. Lily could feel the weight of Andrei's choice, the impossibility of the situation. And yet, he acted, carrying Sebina away in the dead of night, her cries silenced by desperation and the need to protect her.

As it stood, it was an unprecedented move to steal a woman back after she was taken and married. But Andrei was willing to risk punishment and even exile from his own clan.

She was furious and heartbroken. Now, back with her family, they tried to console her, but she was inconsolable. The further they traveled from her child, the more distraught she became, and after months on the road, the rift between the twins grew even wider. Sebina stopped speaking to Andrei, refusing to acknowledge him at all.

Lily swallowed hard, her stomach twisting as she read about the aftermath. Sebina's fury, her heartbreak—Lily felt them as if they were her own.

As time passed, Sebina settled back into clan life and accepted that the odds of ever seeing her son again were slim. Andrei immediately settled back into his own little clan of grifters and soldiers of fortune. And with the animosity that had grown between them and her age, he no longer involved her in his business affairs.

Also, because she had been married and had a child, she was no longer considered "clean" in the eyes of their culture. This meant that, even at her young age, she was no longer seen as an eligible candidate for marriage and would live the compulsory life of a widow.

Restlessness consumed her. Her husband—forced upon her—was gone, and her only child had been taken. Now, relegated to the care of a home and family that were not her own, she knew this life would never fulfill her.

Still young and vibrant, she began to crave a different kind of life—one outside the confines and restrictions of her clan. One she had seen in magazines when she and her mother and cousins shopped in the little towns they would pass through.

The journal's tone shifted again as Andrei described his attempts to repair what he had broken. His guilt propelled him to support Sebina in her quest for a new life, one far from the clan that had failed her.

Through Andrei's eyes, Lily saw Sebina's transformation: a girl hardened by loss, finding strength in her independence. Andrei, feeling responsible for her dispiritedness, promised to help her in any way he could. When the time came, he found a place in Poland where she could start that new life.

He paid for her education and flat while she was in school. Once she completed the equivalent of a high school diploma, she worked in shops and saved her money. At eighteen, she left Poland and landed in Leeds, UK, on her way to London, where she met an Englishman named Frank Thomas.

She fell deeply and madly in love with this boy, and after a short courtship, the two were married and settled in Leeds. After many years of trying to have children, their hopes dashed, a miracle happened, and their only son was born. John Elliot Thomas.

Closing the last of the journals, Lily leaned back, her thoughts racing. The weight of Andrei's choices hung in the air, mingling with the revelations of Sebina's resilience. This wasn't just a story of survival—it was a testament to the sacrifices and scars that shaped their family. As the past settled into place, Lily couldn't shake the feeling that these histories were more than just pieces of a puzzle; they were a mirror, reflecting truths about her own life that she was only beginning to understand.

Chapter Nineteen

Come Back Around

(2021)

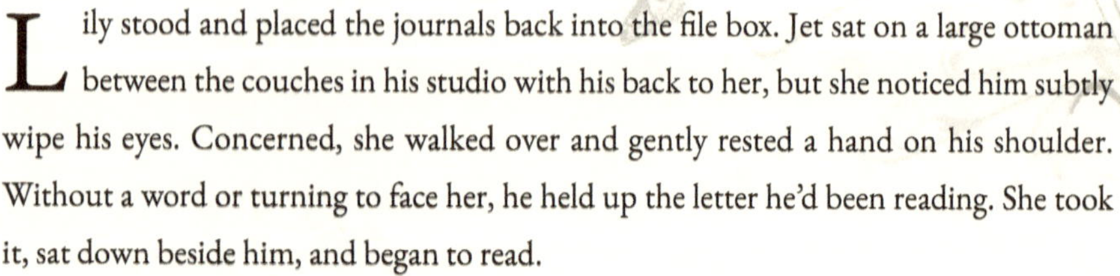

Lily stood and placed the journals back into the file box. Jet sat on a large ottoman between the couches in his studio with his back to her, but she noticed him subtly wipe his eyes. Concerned, she walked over and gently rested a hand on his shoulder. Without a word or turning to face her, he held up the letter he'd been reading. She took it, sat down beside him, and began to read.

My Darling Lily,

If you're reading this, it means I was unable to make things right with you in this life. Since I won't be there to answer your questions, I wanted to explain why I did what I did.

The day your grandparents brought you to England, we were all there to meet you. When you stepped off the plane clutching that worn stuffed bear, your eyes were wide and curious despite the exhaustion etched on your little face. I knew right then you were special. It felt like looking into a mirror of my younger self. Like me, you were a survivor; I could see that in you immediately. You were so sweet, vulnerable, and stubborn—all wrapped up in this tiny fireball of love and sadness.

Please believe me when I say I had no idea you were my granddaughter then. I learned about it the day you told me you might be pregnant.

After you and John left that day, I called my brother, Andrei, who had been planning a visit to discuss troubling news about threats to our clan. He was still in the old country, and I needed to arrange to pick him up when he arrived the following week. During our conversation, I mentioned your situation. That's when Andrei revealed you were Marik's biological daughter and that Emil Daniel—your grandfather and my first husband by kidnapping—had died (or been killed) about a year prior.

The discovery was no accident. My brother, the ever suspicious man that he was, checked the backgrounds of all of John's girlfriends. As he sifted through your background, he uncovered a file buried deeper than he'd expected. What he found shook him—your birth certificate, with Marik's name listed as your father. Of course, this revelation took us aback, knowing the bloodline and dangers we'd escaped all those years ago. Emil was a figure of terrifying significance in his own right—a traumatic bond that still haunts me to this day.

I was twelve when the kidnapping happened. Andrei had just stepped inside a shop, leaving me to sit on a stone wall, when a group of young men grabbed me, put me into a caravan, and whisked me away. When we stopped days later, I was taken to meet Emil, and we were married immediately. Andrei rescued me from the clan three years later, but he couldn't bring the child conceived during that marriage, fearing a clan war.

Emil Daniel was born in Romania and belonged to the Roma royal lineage. After I disappeared from the Daniel clan, we learned Emil took Marik to the U.S. to start over. They settled in northern West Virginia, where a local tribe gave him the title Rom Baro. The people sought someone knowledgeable in Roma traditions and language to stand firm against the Gadjo. Emil fit the role perfectly.

Andrei discovered Marik left the clan in West Virginia and traveled south to Athens, where he met your mother. After their breakup, Marik returned to his clan but later disappeared. There was no trace of him until Emil died and Marik had returned to claim leadership.

Andrei also told me that his rise to power came through violence, coercion, and fear. Those who opposed him were dealt with harshly. Then, when we learned Marik might have discovered you existed, we feared he would use you or Jack to solidify his control over the clan, possibly selling you into servitude or forcing you into a marriage that would further his ambitions. It was a risk we couldn't take, and we needed to move fast.

Trust me, love, the irony is not lost on me: the kidnapping, the loss of family and home ... although I didn't know the details of your abduction or your situation in the States until later, I empathized with the hardship you likely endured.

But the truth, if I'm honest with myself, Lily, was twofold. First, even while trying to protect you from that life, I still failed you in other ways. I know that being forced into a marriage with the young man Andrei chose, even though it wasn't a Romani marriage, was still a betrayal of your autonomy. It broke my heart to make that decision, knowing what I had endured myself. But Andrei said it was the safest way to protect you and Jack from Marik's reach.

But beyond the immediate threat of Marik, Andrei and I also saw the potential for you and Jack to have a life free from the traditions, conflicts, and persecution of our people. I know how limiting that world can be, especially for women. I lived it, and I couldn't bear the thought of you being trapped in a cycle of duty and oppression. You deserved the chance to choose your own path—something I never had until I came to the UK.

Levi had no ties to our clans, and his family's stability offered a shield we couldn't completely provide on our own.

Also, my love, John, wasn't ready to be a father. You and I both know he would've done it—given up his dreams to be there for you. But every time I saw him on stage, pouring his soul into a song, I knew that a life stuck in a factory would've slowly smothered the spark that made him our John.

Among my many regrets, the most unsettling is never telling him about his son, despite coming to terms with my fate and the cancer that will eventually take me. I had hoped John would at least find some peace with Gabriella and build a family with her.

I am grateful for the visits from Andrei and Jack. They meant the world to me, and I believe they were a way for Andrei to make up for losing Marik.

Lily, the decision to hide you was agonizing. I knew it meant keeping you from your heritage, and John, but we truly believed it was the only way. My only consolation was that I made Andrei promise that you and Jack would be free on his eighteenth birthday to follow your hearts, whether that brought you back to us or took you far away. By then, Jack would be old enough to choose his path, and protect you, as an adult and an American citizen.

Again, I am truly sorry things turned out the way they did. I genuinely believed we were working in your best interests. Please don't hold Frank or John responsible; they knew nothing. I love you dearly.

Yours truly, Mum

P.S. We collected a box of files, pictures, and home videos of Jack over the years. Please share them with John. If you're reading this together, I love you, son.

Lily stood abruptly, the letter trembling in her hand before she let it fall into the box. Her breath hitched, and she pressed her palm against her chest as if trying to contain the swell of emotions. "Oh, Mum ... Jesus," she whispered hoarsely, shaking her head. "Talk about the sins of the father."

Her voice cracked, the weight of Mum's words crashing over her. She paced the room, rubbing her arms as though the chill in the air wasn't coming from inside her. Jet watched her, concern etched deep in his eyes. He stepped forward, his hesitation visible, before wrapping his arms around her shoulders. Lily resisted at first, stiff against his embrace, but as the first tears slipped free, she let herself fall into him.

"I can't believe she thought she was saving me," Lily murmured, her voice muffled against Jet's chest. "All those choices she made, thinking it would protect me ... and in the end, I still lived the same nightmare she thought she was saving me from."

Jet's hand stroked her hair, his touch gentle.

"Did you read the whole thing?" she asked after a moment, pulling back just enough to look up at him.

He nodded, his expression shadowed with guilt. "I did," he said. "I'm so sorry, Lily. I never knew any of this. I thought ..." He sighed, his gaze dropping for a moment. "I just thought we were a regular English family."

Lily let out a soft, bitter laugh as she wiped her cheeks with the heel of her hand. "Is there such a thing?" she asked, her tone laced with equal parts sorrow and wry humor.

Jet tilted his head, offering her a faint, sad smile. "Apparently not," he admitted, pulling her close again. "But whatever we are, Lily, we'll figure it out."

For a moment, they stood in silence, the weight of Mum's revelations and the histories in Uncle's journals hanging heavily in the room. Lily's eyes eventually settled on the box sitting on the small end table—a box filled with fragments of a past they were finally starting to piece together. As she rested in Jet's arms, she felt like at least she wasn't facing this completely alone.

Chapter Twenty

Begin again
(2021)

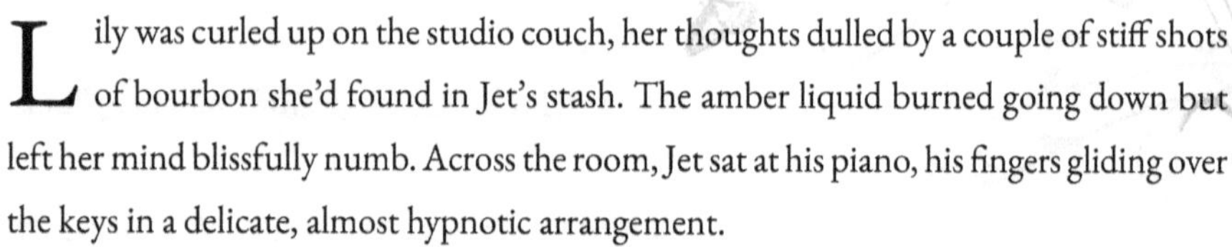

L ily was curled up on the studio couch, her thoughts dulled by a couple of stiff shots of bourbon she'd found in Jet's stash. The amber liquid burned going down but left her mind blissfully numb. Across the room, Jet sat at his piano, his fingers gliding over the keys in a delicate, almost hypnotic arrangement.

"Is that new?" she asked.

He nodded through the intro and then sang.

In silence, alone in your mind,
Your eyes expose the pain left behind.
All of it hidden deep within.
Your soul is waiting to begin again.
And I long to explore every part of you,
Inside and out, let me break through

He stopped playing. "That's all I got so far."

"It's beautiful."

He slid off the piano bench and walked over to her, settling on the couch beside her. Taking her hand in his, he intertwined their fingers and rested them gently on his thigh. She glanced up at him, her eyes shadowed with a wistful expression. "What's on your mind?" he asked softly.

"Nothing in particular. I'm just feeling a little raw right now, trying to process every-thing."

"Yeah."

She shifted closer to him; metal digging into her side as she moved. With a sigh, she leaned forward and pulled the small handgun from her belt. Releasing Jet's hand, she replaced it with the cold weight of the Tomcat. He tried to pull away, but she guided his fingers around the grip.

"It won't hurt you, if you know how to use it."

"Is this really necessary?"

"I don't know. It may be. Better safe than sorry."

She let go of his hand, allowing him to feel the weight of it. He continued to investigate the gun, studying it from all angles. *C'mon, man, it's just a piece of machinery, a tool. Nothing to be afraid of. Don't be a chicken-shit!* He thought to himself, then asked, "I'm not gonna shoot myself, am I?"

She rolled her eyes at him. "The safety's on."

He gave her a weary glance. "Now what?"

She showed him how to tip the barrel up to check the chamber, load the magazine, and where the safety was—then had him point it at a target in the room, keeping his finger off the trigger and resting it along the side.

"It's a small frame pistol, but it can pack a punch. That's what we started Jack with."

"Jack shoots?"

"Babe, when you live on a farm, everybody shoots."

"Yeah, I suppose ..." Holding the weapon reminded him. "Hey, you never told me about this training you went through with my uncle. Is that where you learned all this stuff?"

"Oh, yeah ... well, shooting came from keeping the farm safe. But targeting, tactical weaponry, along with various other skills, came from the training. I told you about the incident with Levi."

"Yeah."

She took a deep breath, looked down, and began. "See, this is why I told you not to make any decisions about us. I mean ... I'm not the same person, Jet. That innocent little girl is gone."

He smiled and continued to aim the gun at different targets, then said, "I know. Now she's more confident, determined, and even more beautiful."

She laughed through her nose and continued, "Hmm, okay ... well, I haven't told you everything ... But it's only fair that you know ... the truth, I mean ... what I'm going to tell you right now may change your mind about everything ... I mean ... It's not good, I'm not good ... anymore—"

He halted her aimless dialog by lowering his face to meet her gaze and locking his eyes with hers. "Lily," he said, his voice unwavering. "After everything we've been through, I seriously doubt anything you say will shock me."

"I killed him ... Levi, I mean. I killed him." She blurted it out there for God and everyone! The deed was done. She'd said it, and she couldn't take it back now! It felt weirdly cathartic, finally saying it out loud, almost like a weight had been lifted. But she had to ask herself if she spit that little nugget of information out there to try to scare him away from a serious relationship again, one she still couldn't entirely trust. Or was it to test her own resolve? Either way, she had just officially given him the perfect excuse to run as fast as he could from her.

Jet's eyes widened with concern. He laid the pistol on the coffee table in front of them, still holding her gaze, grabbed her hands, and said, "Babe, start over. From the beginning, please."

"Okay ... uh." She swallowed hard, dropped her shoulders to calm herself, and began again. "When Jack was ten, I was in the house and heard him scream. I ran outside to find Levi shaking him in the barn. I grabbed the closest thing I could, which was a shovel, and I beat him to death with it. I could have stopped, but I didn't, or maybe I didn't want to. I knew the second he went down that if he recovered, he would retaliate. Against me ... or Jack. So, I just kept beating him until he didn't move anymore." She watched his face as he sat silent, looking for any kind of reaction. But when there wasn't one, she continued, "I told him the last time he slapped Jack that if he ever touched him again, I would kill him. At the time, it felt like more of a threat. I didn't think I meant it, but ... anyway, it all played out in slow motion. My training kicked in, I guess. I didn't even have to think. I knew where to strike for maximum damage, and when I was done ... I called Uncle and told him to come."

"Where was Jack?"

"Oh, yeah, sorry. I sent him into the house as soon as Levi let go of him. Jesus, Jet, I'm not a monster."

Jet sat back in relief and said, "What did my uncle do?"

"Well, when he got there, he put Levi in the trunk of his car. We heard him moan, so he wasn't completely dead yet."

"So, how do you know you killed him?"

"Does it matter—whether I killed him there in the barn, or whether he died on the way to wherever Uncle took him, or even if Uncle finished him off, I intended to kill him at that moment. He died because of me. Anyway, we never saw Levi again.

"When Jack asked about him, I didn't go into detail. I just said that he went away and wasn't coming home. He never questioned me again after that. Maybe Uncle talked to him about it, I don't know."

"Lil, that sounds more like self-defense. You were protecting our child. But honestly, I'm more concerned with this training you've talked about. Was my uncle trying to turn you into some kind of soldier or one of his MERCs?"

"Wait? So, it doesn't bother you that I'm responsible for another human being's death?"

"Not that one. If Levi were still alive, I'd have liked to kill him myself for what he put you through."

"Well, I presume that's kinda where Uncle's mindset was. I think the training was more for our protection when he wasn't around. And you know what's really strange? I could never quite figure him out.

"Despite all the threats he made, regardless of how angry he was with me, no matter how many times I ran away or refused to follow his orders, he never physically harmed Jack or me. In fact, he became more kind to us over time.

"When I finally agreed to undergo training, he installed the landline phone for local calls only, to ensure we had a way to communicate.

"Ya know when he got to the house after I called him about Levi, his first words were … he was surprised it took me so long. Honestly, I think he would have been dead long before that if I had told Uncle everything, but, at the time, I still didn't know who I could trust. I didn't know if he and Levi were connected in some way, what their relationship was, or why this particular man was chosen for me. So, I just kept quiet. I mean, why waste your breath telling on your captor's hired hand, right?

"But the doctor, I mean Lavina knew for sure. She saw the evidence … I don't know if she ever said anything, though. The funny part is even though I never said anything, Andrei didn't particularly care for Levi. He believed him to be 'weak of mind'; I heard him say once. Like I said, I think he wanted us to train because of that, so I wasn't weak … so Jack wasn't weak." She shrugged. "But knowing what we know now, I guess it makes sense. He was just taking care of his family, literally."

Chapter Twenty-One

Hidey Holes

(2021)

"Where did he train you?"

"Remember the warehouse I told you about." Jet nodded. "Mostly there. While Levi did morning chores or slept off the night before, Uncle or the doctor would pick us up several mornings of the week before Jack had to be at school. We would warm up by running and doing muscle-building workouts. Then, someone would take Jack to school, and he would run me through scenarios.

"Drills like, if an assailant attacks from behind or has a knife or how to run from gunfire … did you know that if you run from someone firing at you, the odds of them hitting you in a vital area drop to about 25%."

"No shit?"

"Yeah, so if someone is shooting at you, RUN!" she snorted. "Anyway … after Levi was … gone … he thought I was ready, so I went on small ops with him and his team. Mostly protection details."

"Protection details? What, like a bodyguard or something?"

She rolled her eyes at him. "Or something," she continued, "When important people, to him, would come into town, we would scout the locations, where they would stay or visit, that kind of stuff. And when I say important, I don't mean good people—more like influential in his line of work, important.

"We met a few Senators a couple of times. But most of them were all underworld-type bosses or, knowing what we know now, possibly other Rom Baros from different clans."

"Did you ever have to fight or shoot anyone?"

"I've never had to shoot at anyone … but fights?" She shrugged. "Sure, I mean, it was more restraint-type situations, though, breaking up fights after meetings, that sort of thing. I don't think he would have had me on any detail that would have put me in any real danger, ya know. I think he saved those jobs for his hired help.

"Sometimes, while waiting for my ride home after my training, I would watch the others go through their drills. And I am sure they were training for much more dangerous operations."

"What the hell kind of business was my uncle into?"

"I wasn't privy to any details, but if I had to guess, by what I read in his journals earlier, I believe he was an entrepreneurial opportunist who sold his team's services. Like for security or even MERC type stuff, to whomever was willing to pay."

"Were you ever scared on any of these Ops?"

She thought for a moment. "I think what Uncle was trying to instill in me and Jack was the ability to work through your fear. If you train long enough for a situation, you're ready. You won't freeze or take flight; you could face it."

"Yeah, but you can't train for everything."

"No, but you can learn skills to help you in those circumstances."

"Like what?"

"Okay, well, for example, when you walk into a strange place, do you pay attention to your surroundings?"

"Yeah, I guess."

"Okay, you've been to the pub a lot, right?"

"Yeah, I basically live there when I'm home."

"Do you know where all the exits are? Will the windows open, or are they fixed? Do you know where the hidey holes are or areas that can be used as such?"

"Hidey holes?"

Getting a little frustrated. "C'mon Jet. Hiding places. Answer the question. Do you know your surroundings?"

He didn't respond, confirming his absolute lack of awareness, so she continued, "Like, this is the first time I have ever been in your home. I can tell you where every exit is, every escape route, every place that can be used as a shelter in case of flying bullets ... you live here. Do you know these?"

"Jesus, Lil."

"It's so I don't have to think. I already know and can react or defend instead of wasting precious time trying to figure those things out."

She stood up and began pacing around the room. Grabbing an electrical cord, she held it up to him. "Obviously, you're no electrician because this extension cord should not be used for this type of appliance. It's designed for a lamp or something small, not a mini-fridge. It's pulling too much of a load, and it's warm to the touch."

"This is a huge fire hazard, Jet. You need to change it. Lucky for you, I'm not the fire inspector, but for the purpose of this conversation, I would not pick this cord to grab and use to tie someone up or try to subdue them with it."

"Why?"

"Because it's warm, and my target could easily break or stretch it." She continued to walk around the studio. She pointed out the one whole wall that was ceiling-to-floor windows, looking out over a beautiful paddock with a couple of grazing horses, then another wall covered in framed albums and awards, then a third corner with a glass enclosure for the drums and a microphone. "Lots of glass in here, none of it tempered. Bullets, rocks, hell, any heavy object could shatter it all, creating a fine dusting of glass shards.

"This is not a room I would take shelter in. But the main house, on the other hand, is solid stone. I noticed a floor panel in your butler's pantry. I'm pretty sure it leads to a crawl space under the house. If we were to be infiltrated, that is where I would send everyone."

"When the hell did you have time to figure all this out?"

"It doesn't take that long if you know what to look for. Besides, you were showing everyone around, and while they were looking at the decor and making sure they knew where the bathrooms were, I was planning an escape route if necessary."

"Well, thank you, Uncle Andrei." He smiled acrimoniously.

He got up, walked over, and grabbed her around her waist. She put her arms around his neck as he leaned in to kiss her. "You're kind of a badass, babe."

She laughed through her nose, shaking her head, and said, "No, just trained." She gave him another quick kiss, then pulled away. "I lost my shit the day you walked back into my life, remember? Training didn't help me that day. Lavina was right. I let my guard down because I was here in the UK and felt like I was safe. It won't happen again."

As she attempted to step back away from him, she caught a glimpse of movement in her periphery, outside the studio window. "Don't look out the window. Keep your eyes on me and follow my lead."

She took one of his hands from her waist and led him toward the studio door, slyly picking the Tomcat up from the coffee table as they passed. Once they were in the hall, she dropped his hand and tipped up the barrel to check for ammo. She crouched down a bit, pushing him behind her, then strolled to a vantage point where she could see the rest of the property. She noticed several vehicles lining the drive, then caught a group of people carrying duffle bags and what looked like cases of equipment walking in their direction.

"What is it? What do you see?" Jet's query was just above a whisper.

Taking her first breath, in what seemed like a full minute, she clicked the safety on the pistol, placed it into the hollow of her back, and stood straight.

"It's nothing ..." She nodded toward the glass door. "Looks like the security team Lavina sent is here."

"How do you know?"

"Because, if they were here to cause harm, they wouldn't be walking in a group straight down the center of the drive, nor would they have let themselves be seen."

"So we're good?"

"Good? That remains to be seen ..." She eyed the group. "Safe? Probably ... at least for the moment."

They left the studio and walked out to meet the group. Jet and Lily showed them back to the studio and helped them get settled. They informed Lily of Lavina's ETA and got to work.

Jet took them to his Head-end closet, now designated as the armory. It was significantly oversized considering the limited audio and security equipment Jet housed. It had a dedicated cooling system, making it the most appropriate place for the team's provisions.

Lily made her way to the main house to get Ana and bring her to the studio for a debrief and planning session.

Ana was tall, well, everyone was tall compared to Lily, but Ana was unusually tall for a woman. At least six foot three with a solid, husky frame. Lily figured that was why Jet hired her. She guessed Ana could easily lift his father, Frank, if needed. Now, knowing that she worked with Andrei and Lavina, she believed she had been sent more for protection and to spy.

Ana wore her dark brown hair in a tight bun at the nape and looked to be around forty. She never saw her wear any makeup, but her skin was smooth and caramel in color. Usually, she wore scrubs to the house to work with Frank, but since everyone knew her secret now, and she was doing double duty, she wore a black fitted pantsuit that was evidently made to stretch and conceal weapons. Lily actually felt a little safer knowing this woman was on their side.

Walking back into the studio, they saw a familiar face. Viktor, the lead male team member standing in the middle of the studio ready to begin. "We have about three hours until Lavina and the Stratton family arrive." He pulled out a satellite map of Jet's compound and directed each member to a location for surveillance.

Lily chimed in, "Excuse me, what exactly are we looking for?"

"Anything out of the ordinary, for right now."

"And that would be? Since this is the first time we've all been here," she said, slightly exasperated.

"Mrs. Stratton, you let us worry about that," Viktor said smugly.

Pissed at being referred to as 'Mrs. Stratton,' Lily approached the man, intending to confront him, but Jet grabbed her arm. When she looked back at him, his face showed concern. Not wanting to add to that by causing a scene, she stepped back.

Clearly, they did not consider her part of the team, but rather the subject of their detail, and it irked her. This was her family, for God's sake, and if Andrei were around, she would give him an ear full right about now.

Lily had had enough. She relented and then snapped, "Let me know when Lavina and the kids get here!"

"Yes, Ma'am!"

She and Jet turned to leave. "Mr. Thomas, a moment, please?"

Jet stopped at the team leader's request and turned back to tell Lily, "I'll meet you back at the house."

"It'll only take a few minutes," the team leader reassured her.

She nodded and headed out of the room.

Instead of heading straight to the house, Lily sat on the bench outside the studio, letting the warm breeze brush against her skin as she admired the vibrant hues of Jet's garden. A walk around the property seemed like a good way to settle her nerves and get a clearer sense of their surroundings. She couldn't help but wonder about the layout—how far the property stretched and how secure it really was. The wooded forest surrounding the compound looked beautiful, but also made her question if it could shield more than just nature.

From her spot on the bench, she could see the entrance and the drive where several of Lavina's security team's vehicles parked. The circular drive looped elegantly from the studio to the house, with a large stone fountain in the center and a short hedge framing the inner circle like a natural barrier.

The drive was broad, wide enough for cars to park in a neat line while others passed easily around them. Beyond the drive, the thick woods seemed to encircle them entirely, its edges blurring into the horizon. She couldn't tell exactly where Jet's property ended—or how well-guarded it might be. The thought settled uneasily in her mind.

When Jet finally emerged from the studio, Lily stood and offered a small smile, brushing her hands on her jeans.

"You waited," he said with a warm smile, slipping his hands into his pockets as he approached.

"Of course," she replied lightly. "I was enjoying the garden—and I thought maybe we could take a walk? Around the property, I mean. It looks like there's a lot to see."

He tilted his head, a curious look crossing his face. "A walk, huh? Thinking of something specific?"

She hesitated, choosing her words carefully. "Not really specific. I just ... thought it'd be good to stretch my legs. And honestly, I'd like to know how everything's set up out here. It seems private, but it's so big."

Jet nodded, his expression softening with understanding. "You're wondering about hidey holes."

Lily grinned and shrugged, not wanting to overstate it but also not wanting to lie. She held up her hand, her thumb and finger just barely apart, as if measuring an invisible thread. "Maybe just a little. It's gorgeous, but it feels ... open."

"It's more secure than it looks," he assured her, his voice steady. "I can show you as we walk. You'll see where the boundaries are and how everything's connected."

She smiled again, some of the tension easing from her shoulders. "I'd like that."

Jet grabbed Lily's hand as they started along the looping drive toward the house. A van turned into the drive and rumbled toward them.

"Looks like more team members," Jet said, squinting toward the vehicle.

The van screeched to a halt, tires kicking up a spray of gravel as the side door slid open. Before it even stopped moving, three hooded men launched out. The two largest figures converged on Jet, gripping his arms like iron vises as he twisted and shoved, his muscles straining against their hold. "Get off me!" he roared. Jet's thrashing made him a tough target, and he managed to get one arm free, allowing his fist to make contact with the larger man's jaw. The second man surged back into action and was able to regain control of Jet. They yanked him toward the van with brutal precision.

A third assailant closed in on Lily from behind, his movements predatory. His rough hands latched onto her arms, but Lily reacted with the instincts of a cornered lioness. Her heel came down hard on his foot, the crunch of bone audible over his startled grunt. Spinning with precision, she delivered a sharp punch to his face; the force snapping his head back. Without hesitation, her knee followed up, connecting squarely with his groin. The man folded like a book, collapsing to his knees, gasping for air.

Lily's breaths came quick and shallow, but she didn't stop. As her attacker swayed, trying to steady himself, she lunged, her fist cracking against his temple. He dropped onto his stomach, groaning, but she wasn't finished. Another kick to his ribs sent him sprawling.

Backing away, she reached for the gun tucked at her waist. Her hands were steady as she drew it, her eyes narrowing with cold precision. The man stumbled back to his feet, but Lily squeezed the trigger. The deafening crack echoed as the bullet slammed into his leg, sending him toppling with a howl of pain.

Her aim shifted to the van. The man holding the door open barely had time to register the threat before she fired again; the shot grazed his shoulder and knocked him backward into the vehicle. Chaos erupted inside as his comrades scrambled to react.

"Lily, run!" Jet's voice came strained, his struggle growing desperate as the remaining men shoved him closer to the van.

Lily swung her aim toward Jet's captors, her sights locking on the one dragging him. Before she could pull the trigger, the driver leaped out of the van and slammed into her with full force. They hit the ground in a tangle of limbs as the gun went off; the round ricocheting inside the van and sparking against the passenger seat.

Pain seared through her side as the driver tried to pin her. Gritting her teeth, she thrashed beneath him, trying to aim her pistol into the side of her attacker. Clawing and kicking with everything she had, she couldn't get a clear shot, as his weight was overwhelming. Her voice was raw with defiance as she shouted, "Let. Him. Go!"

The shots and struggle had alerted the team inside the building. Doors burst open, Lavina's team pouring out with guns drawn, but the attackers moved with practiced speed. Jet was already inside the van, his voice shouting her name over the commotion.

The man on the ground scrambled back to his feet, dragging himself toward the van, clutching his injured leg. Lily's chest heaved as she weighed her options, her mind racing. Jet was out of reach. If she continued to fight now, she might lose her only chance to stay with him.

"Okay! Okay!" she screamed, her voice cutting through the chaos. Lily's hands went up in surrender as she dropped her gun, letting the man pull her up and toward the van. Her knees buckled as they shoved her inside, but she didn't resist. Her heart thundered as she looked back at the studio's door, Lavina's team rushing forward, weapons raised and ready to fire, but it was too late.

They watched as the doors to the van closed. Lily and Jet remained subdued while the vehicle sped off the property. Several team members ran to vehicles to pursue, while others ran to the main house to check for intruders. Viktor and the second in command explored the area where the fight took place, finding Lily's gun.

"Looked like she went willingly," Viktor said.

The second in command replied, "Good thing they wanted them alive."

"Yeah, c'mon, I need to make some calls."

Chapter Twenty-Two

Party Time
(2021)

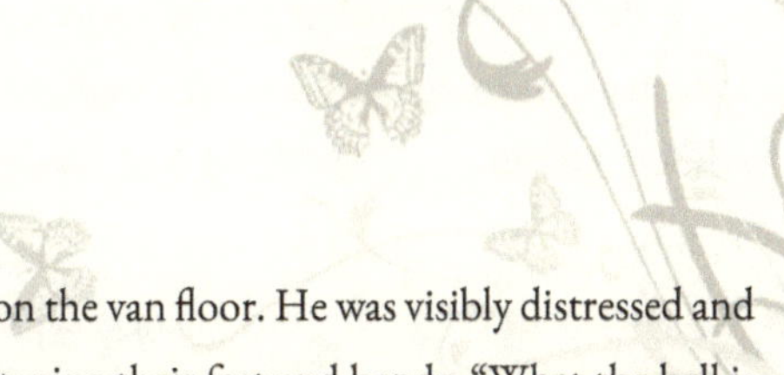

Lily and Jet sat across from each other on the van floor. He was visibly distressed and yelled at the captors while they were taping their feet and hands. "What the hell is going on here!? Where are you taking us?"

No response came as he looked over at Lily. She met his gaze with the slightest shake of her head, effectively telling him to stop talking.

He complied, maintaining his focus on her. She gave him a comforting wink, then closed her eyes, taking a deep breath in through her nose. Holding it for a moment, she then exhaled through her mouth. Her eyes widened, and she raised her eyebrows encouragingly. With a quick nod, she repeated the process, and Jet caught on, following suit. She needed him to stay calm if they were going to think clearly and find a way out of this situation.

"We're being followed!" the driver said.

"Well, lose them!" the passenger yelled.

The driver shot back, "No shit?!" yanking the wheel hard to the left. Sudden turns sent everyone in the back sprawling against the walls of the van. The two men Lily had shot groaned loudly, their pained protests barely audible over the squeal of tires.

The pursuing car closed the distance, headlights glaring in the van's side mirrors. A loud *thud* reverberated as the chase vehicle rammed their rear bumper.

"Hold on!" the driver barked, slamming his foot on the gas. The van surged forward, weaving between slower cars on the motorway. Jet and Lily tried to brace themselves against the van's walls as it swayed violently.

"They're still on us!" the passenger shouted, twisting to peer through the rear window.

"I can see that!" the driver snarled, exiting the motorway and cutting through the intersection just as the light turned red. The pursuers followed, narrowly avoiding a collision with a truck that blared its horn.

The crack of gunfire pierced the air, and the van's side mirror exploded in shards.

"What the hell? They know we have their people, right?!" the driver cursed, jerking the wheel to send the van swerving into an alley. "This thing isn't built for this shit!" he yelled, barely avoiding a dumpster as sparks flew from the van's side, scraping against the wall.

As the alley narrowed, the pursuers were forced to hold back, giving the van a fleeting advantage. Bursting onto the main road, the driver veered into oncoming traffic, leaving chaos in his wake as horns blared, brakes screeched, and cars swerved desperately to avoid a collision.

"They're backing off!" the passenger called, relief creeping into his voice.

The van barreled forward, engine straining under the relentless abuse as the driver made another sharp turn, narrowly missing a pedestrian. It looked like the pursuing car was struggling to keep up, the gap between them widening.

Finally, after what felt like an eternity, the pursuing car disappeared.

"I think we lost 'em!" the driver announced triumphantly, pulling into a secluded side street, entering a garage and cutting the engine. Everyone inside the van slumped against the walls, breathing heavily.

When the van finally stilled, the rear doors swung open, revealing a large man with a bright smile. Half of his long, salt-and-pepper hair was tied back, while the rest flowed freely down the middle of his back. Small gold hoop earrings glinted in his ears, and a neatly trimmed, graying beard and mustache framed his face.

Lily glared hard at the man, but there was something familiar about him. His eyes were big and bright green with a deep blue rim around the iris; these eyes were the same as Jets, the same as hers. Lily recognized the familial resemblance.

The man looked at the bindings. "This is unnecessary; free them!"

Lily dropped her chin, shaking her head, and then looked up at him. "Marik?"

The man clapped once, threw his hands in the air, and exuberantly yelled, "AH! She knows her Papa!"

Two men cut their bindings as the driver, and others helped carry the injured men out of the van. Marik barked another command, "Take them to the doctor."

Then he waved his hands at Jet and Lily, gesturing for them to follow him. "Come ... come, you must meet everyone!" They looked at each other hesitantly as they inched to the end of the van and hopped out.

Jet grabbed Lily's hand and pulled her close, embodying the protective man she knew and loved. She clung to his arm with her other hand, glancing up at him as he led her forward. It was clear he was now taking her "pay attention" speech to heart, and she, too, was vigilant, keenly taking stock of their surroundings.

The driver had pulled the van into a parking garage. Lily recognized the area. They were in Leeds. Actually, not that far from her Aunt Minnie and Frank's house. She squeezed Jet's hand and got his attention. He looked back at her as they walked, and she gestured for him to look over the parking wall. He recognized where he was, too, then looked down at her to confirm.

The building they were walking into was an apartment complex, but they were headed for something other than elevators. They were being steered toward a common area, where they heard loud music and what sounded like a large number of people gathered together.

Marik led them through a set of double doors where a party was most certainly taking place. He turned to Lily and Jet with his hands wide, gesturing for them to enter.

Once inside, he clapped loudly, and the crowd quieted. "Everyone!" he yelled excitedly. "I want you to meet my lovely daughter and newfound brother!" Everyone cheered as the music blared again.

Marik walked behind them and wrapped his arms around their shoulders, guiding them to a low-sitting banquet table surrounded by vibrant, colorful pillows. He took his place at the head of the table and gestured for them to sit, one on each side, facing each other.

The table was lavishly set, with at least twenty place settings along the sides, and an array of dishes lined the center in an opulent display. The room was filled with more tables, similarly adorned, and at the front, a dance floor filled with party guests enjoying the festivities.

"Marik, what's going on?" Lily spoke first.

"Can't a man celebrate finding his long-lost family?"

"An invitation would have sufficed. What the hell is it with you people and abductions?"

Marik's eyes sparkled with mischief as he motioned toward the tables laden with food and drink. "It is our way … come now, enjoy!" he urged, his voice light with laughter. With a wave of his hand, a woman approached, bowing her head respectfully. Marik leaned in close, whispering something in her ear, too softly for Lily to catch. The woman nodded without hesitation, then slipped away into the crowd, vanishing into the lively celebration as Marik turned back to them with a grin.

A minute later, the room quieted as more people entered. It was Jack and Renee being led by Lavina.

Angry now. "Really, Marik, what is going on?" Lily tried to stand, but Marik held her and Jet's arms to keep them seated.

"All will be explained in due time, my dear." He then pointed at the seats he wanted his new guests to sit in. Renee and Jack sat next to Jet on his side and Lavina beside Lily.

Lily mouthed to Jack, "Are you okay?" He nodded but did not indicate his state of mind. She scrutinized him, searching his face for any sign of emotion. His eyes were void, betraying nothing. Was he scared? Angry? Or was he putting his training to work?

She remembered their conversation about him already knowing who Lavina was, then wondered if this had all been planned. Had they corrupted him somehow? No, absolutely not. This was her son. She knew him. He couldn't be involved in this. Could he? Questions swirled in her mind, growing more urgent by the second, her training fueling her suspicion.

She turned her attention back to Jet, his jaw clenched tight as if he were fighting to keep his emotions in check. He took a shaky breath, shoulders rising and falling unevenly. Lily wanted to comfort him, hold his hand, touch him in some way, but she obviously could not move from her seat. So she gave him a reassuring half-smile. It didn't relieve his distress, but he returned the smile. That would have to do for now.

The music stopped abruptly as someone at the podium spoke in Romani; everyone scattered from the dance floor and sat at the various tables. Hot foods were being served as people chatted amongst themselves. Marik's table, however, was considerably less talkative. Lily sat, picking at her plate and watching the rest of her family eat in silence.

Finally, cutting the tension, Marik spoke. "Is everything to your liking?" He looked around the table for responses. Everyone nodded except for Lily and Lavina. Lily took a large gulp of her wine, finishing the glass. Marik called a server over to refill it as he looked over the table.

His attention was now on the other side of the room as he excused himself and stood. They stared at Marik suspiciously.

Lily leaned slightly over to Lavina and asked, "What happened?"

"This is not the time."

"I would say this is exactly the time."

"No more wine; you need to keep a clear head."

"That wine is the only thing keeping me from jumping up and—"

Marik sat back at the table and declared, "Now we can talk about business."

Several other men joined them, filling the rest of the seats at the table. "Daria. Jack. These are my lieutenants. They are here to help you acclimate to your new positions. As my progeny, you are now the heir to my throne and all I own." Marik held up his wineglass to toast. "We are family, and family takes care of family." Everyone in the room cheered and clinked glasses.

Lily looked at Lavina, who showed no sign of emotion. *Always the stoic.* Then she looked back at Marik. He stood and spoke directly to Jack and Daria, "Please, walk with me, and let's talk. It's very loud here."

Lavina, Jet, and Renee looked very concerned about their departure from the table, but Jack and Daria complied with his request. It was the only way Daria felt she would get any answers.

They followed Marik into the garage and over to a set of elevators that took them up four floors to an apartment. "This is my cousin's home. He has allowed me to use it while he is at the horse fair. Please come in."

He directed them in and offered them a seat on the couch as he sat across from them in a chair. "Jack, how was your trip? Pleasant, I hope?"

Before Jack could answer, Daria spoke, "Marik, please get to the point. What's the meaning of all this?"

"Ah, right to the point, then. Daria, my dear, how much do you know of our family?"

"Just what I've read recently in some old files that the Marin's kept."

"And what information did they have about me?"

"I know you are my biological father and that you may or may not have known that Joanna was pregnant when you broke up. I also know that John's mother, Sebina, was your mother, too, and that Andrei Marin abducted her ... after, of course, she was kidnapped by Emil's family and forced to marry him. Oh, and you claimed Rom Baro after your father passed. But that's about it."

"Well, you have the facts but let me tell you the full story of your family."

Marik got up and stood by the small window of the cramped apartment, a cigarette burning between his fingers. The smell of smoke curled through the air, mingling with the faint scent of old leather and coffee. He glanced out at the street below, his gaze distant. Daria and Jack sat across from him, still perched on the couch behind a scarred wooden coffee table. They waited, silent, as Marik exhaled a cloud of smoke and began to speak.

"My father," he said, his voice rough and low, "was once a promising young man. Emil Daniel, a name that once carried weight in our world, born into the prominent Daniel clan. He was a cousin to Alexei Boswell—'King of the Gypsies'—a man of great influence and power. From the beginning, Emil was expected to rise through the family ranks, to honor the Boswell name, just as Alexei had. But..."

Marik paced the length of the room, running a hand through his unruly hair. "But my father wasn't like Alexei. He had a restless spirit, a wild streak that couldn't be tamed. The weight of expectations suffocated him, and instead of rising to meet them, he rebelled. While Alexei became a leader, admired and respected, my father ... let his envy consume him."

He smashed his cigarette into an overflowing ashtray and lit another in a smooth, practiced motion.

"Emil turned to a different life. What started as minor crimes—a horse here, a wagon there—became a full commitment to thievery. He joined a band of rogues, forsaking the honor of our family. At first, I think he told himself it was just to survive, but over time, survival wasn't enough. He wanted more. He wanted Alexei's power, his respect."

Marik's pacing grew restless, his steps echoing softly on the worn floorboards. He paused near the table, leaning on it as his eyes met Daria's. "Do you know what it's like to be cast out? To lose everything?"

"To lose everything? Yeah, I actually do." Daria admitted with as much disdain as she could muster.

Marik's voice wavered for a moment, then steadied. "Well, when Emil's crimes became too much to ignore, the family turned their backs on him. Alexei disowned him, stripped him of his name, his honor. They left him with nothing."

Jack shifted uncomfortably in his chair, but Marik didn't seem to notice. He straightened and began pacing again, his free hand gesturing sharply. "Penniless and desperate, my father concocted a plan—a foolish, desperate plan. He learned of Sebina Marin, a young woman promised to another Boswell cousin. Her dowry and status could have been his salvation. So he did what desperate men do—he took her."

Daria's eyes narrowed, and Marik's gaze softened briefly. "Yes," he said quietly, "he kidnapped her, believing a forced marriage contract would give him a way back into the family. But he underestimated Andrei, Sebina's brother. Andrei wasn't just loyal—he was relentless. For three years, he hunted my father, refusing to rest until he found her."

Marik took a deep drag of his cigarette and blew it out before continuing. "Andrei succeeded. One morning, Emil woke to find Sebina gone. It broke him. Not because he loved her—no, my father didn't know love. But because she was his last chance. Without her, there was no path back to the family, no way to reclaim his name."

The cigarette in his hand burned down to the filter, and Marik stubbed it out with a harsh twist. "So he ran. He took me, and we fled to America. A new land, a fresh start ... or so he thought. But you can't really outrun your past, can you?

"As it happened, and in spite of all that, for a time, he became a revered and successful man in the States. This was mainly due to his vast knowledge of our people's old ways and traditions and, of course, our royal lineage. He shared this knowledge with the clans of West Virginia, where we settled, and they enjoyed prosperity under his guidance.

"They gave him the title of Rom Baro and we lived a life of luxury akin to that of kings. But, as time went on, my fathers greed grew, and the gifts and tithes he received were no longer enough to sustain his extravagant lifestyle. Consequently, he returned to his old ways, leading him down a path of trickery and duplicity once again.

"That is when I left." Marik stood, walked to the kitchen bar, and pulled yet another cigarette out of the pack. He lit it, pulled in a deep drag. Squinting as smoke curled around his face. He exhaled and walked back over to sit down again. "My father lived and died a thief, a failure, a disgrace. And I've spent my life trying to be something more than the shadow of his mistakes."

Marik stood and walked back over to the window, looking out again, as if he were searching for something. Jack and Daria waited patiently for him to continue. Then he turned to face them fully, his voice dropping to a near whisper.

"I was sixteen at the time and ended up in the Athens area. That's where I met Joanna. You favor her, you know."

"That's what they say," Lily responded.

Marik pulled out a chair from the small dinette and sat facing them. "She, too, was sixteen, and I had never met anyone so beautiful. Not just her looks, but her soul. She was sweet, and kind, and forgiving, especially of me.

"Oh, her parents were not happy about her choosing a vagrant boyfriend, but she loved me just the same, and they, being the kind-hearted people they were, took me in until ..."

He stood again, crushing his half-smoked cigarette on the dish placed on the coffee table between them, and then walked back over to the window, searching, this time his face reacted as if he recognized something or someone and said, "My father found me and took advantage of the situation. Of course, he would ruin that, too.

"He started in the Atlanta area with a Ponzi Scheme of sorts. Using his title to manipulate unsuspecting Romani people and others, then worked his way to Athens, eventually catching up to me. His investments were bogus and by the time he got to Joanna's parents the scheme was falling apart.

"Wallace, a clever man, quickly caught on, and thinking that I was somehow involved in the scheme, well, he immediately threw me out. He forbade Joanna from ever seeing me again. Wallace contacted the authorities, so Emil fled, forcing me to go with him."

Marik turned to face them, his expression softening. "I loved your mother deeply, but it was for the best," he said, his voice tinged with regret. "Emil would have made her life hell. I didn't want that for her. Joanna may have been of Roma descent, but her family did not follow the old ways. She was a free spirit and would never have found happiness in this world.

"I was not aware that she was with child at the time." He looked at Daria convincingly. "Sometime after we returned to West Virginia, I left my father again and roamed for years. I roamed from place to place, finding odd jobs and odd friends." He laughed through his nose at the thought of them.

"It wasn't until after my fathers death that I discovered I had a child," Marik continued, his voice steady but laced with a hint of sadness. "I came across an article about the shooting in his papers, and then, finding her obituary that said she was survived by a daughter, I tried to locate you.

"Fortunately for me, your grandfather put your name and age in the obituary. But the trail grew cold when you turned eighteen.

"I must say, Andrei did an impressive job of hiding you all these years. But he made one crucial mistake by not changing your first name. After my father's passing, I inherited the position of Rom Baro."

"You mean you *took* the position!" Jack interjected, his voice sharp with accusation.

"Well, that is a matter of opinion. Regardless, it was then that I was granted access to a network of skilled individuals who spent a considerable amount of time searching all over Europe and America. I will tell you, finding you my dear, was no simple task. John was easy enough to find. My mothers records were quickly discovered and then, as technology and databases became more readily available, they finally discovered the correct state; fortunately the county you resided in finally went digital and only a few Darias of your age were in the public records. It didn't take long after that to locate the property. Further investigation determined that you had already left the States. We figured you would head home, and after speaking with your aunt and conducting a little more surveillance, well, here we are."

Daria's eyes narrowed as she questioned, "But why the abduction and all the vainglory? Why not just contact us?"

Marik exhaled a plume of smoke and extinguished it, before responding, "I told you, this is how it is done. I could not risk you refusing my request for a meeting."

Daria's tone sharpened. "Well, you got your meeting. We're literally your captive audience. So why are we here?"

Marik walked back to the kitchen bar, retrieving yet another cigarette. "Times are changing, my dear," he said, tilting his head to light it. "My people are moving toward a more modern way of life. They would rather pay taxes than tithes. And now my influence wanes as cities grow larger and the Gorger grows less accommodating to our way of life. In essence, the King is asking for more while the people give less, and I am caught in the middle with no way out."

Jack, sensing the shift in Marik's tone, leaned forward and asked, "I thought you were the king?"

"No, Rom Baro means big man; I am more of a governor. Sure, I have power and title at home, but our King lives here in Yorkshire."

"And you're telling us this, why?" Lily asked.

"I had no choice but to embrace the very thing I was trying to avoid—becoming my father. As a governor, the King has certain expectations in the form of tithes and gifts, but I can no longer meet these demands. Nevertheless, I have crafted a plan to solve these problems."

"And I take it that's where we come in?" Lily remarked.

Marik's phone rang, cutting the tension with its abrupt sound. He glanced at the screen, his expression unreadable, then answered with a low murmur. Jack and Daria exchanged uneasy glances, unable to make out the words but picking up on the urgency in Marik's tone. He responded with clipped phrases, his eyes flicking briefly toward them before returning to the call.

After a few tense moments, he hung up and let out a long breath, rubbing his temples. "It appears that my timeline has been moved up," he said, his voice grave.

Jack tensed. "And that concerns us, how, exactly?"

Marik took a slow drag of his cigarette, exhaling smoke as if weighing his next words carefully. "Let's just say that your arrival was more than timely. The wheels have already been set in motion."

Lily spoke up, her eyes narrowing. "Why do I get the feeling we're not going to like where this is headed?"

Marik tilted his head, a shadow of a smile crossing his face. "I had hoped to ease you into it, but I suppose circumstances demand a swifter approach." He paused, his gaze steady and penetrating. "I have a proposition—one that, if accepted, will solve many problems. For all of us."

Daria crossed her arms, eyes steely. "And if we refuse?"

Marik's smile faded, replaced by a look that was equal parts resignation and resolve. "I sincerely hope you won't."

Chapter Twenty-Three

Sometimes You Gotta Cut and Run (2021)

Meanwhile, back at the table where Jet, Renee, and Lavina were seated, anxiously waiting, one of Marik's lieutenants discreetly pulled out his phone to make a call. His voice was low, almost drowned out by the lively atmosphere around them. After a brief conversation, he ended the call and slid the phone back into his pocket.

Standing up, he walked to the head of the table and addressed the three of them, his tone curt but respectful. "Please, follow me."

Jet, sensing the tension in the air, frowned and asked, "Where are we going?"

The lieutenant's expression remained neutral as he replied, "To meet your loved ones."

Jet, Renee, and Lavina rose from their seats and followed the man as he led them out of the room. Walking in a single file, Jet led the way, followed by Renee and then Lavina. One lieutenant escorted them while another followed closely behind. They went through the garage and entered a hallway filled with doors, three of which were open. Armed men guarded each of the open doors.

Lavina stopped short when she noticed them. The lieutenant behind her grabbed her arms, pinning them to her side as he pushed her slim frame forward. Jet paused as he heard the commotion behind him. Realizing they might be in danger, he turned, grabbed Renee, and attempted to get her out of harm's way. But the men were already on them, holding them and shoving each into a separate door, locking it.

Jet's fists slammed against the door, the sound echoing in the confined space. His heart raced as he struggled to adjust his eyes to the near-complete darkness. The only glimmer of light came from the crack at the bottom of the door, but seconds later, even that was gone.

He could hear Renee's desperate cries as she pleaded, "Help! Somebody, please, help us!"

"Quiet, child!" Lavina's voice was firm. "You must stay calm. Panicking will help no one."

Jet's mind raced as he fumbled through his pockets, finding his lighter. Flicking it open, the flame lit up the cramped room. They had been tossed into storage closets. The claustrophobic space was barely big enough to stretch his arms out. The walls were unpainted concrete, rough and cold to the touch, with faint graffiti scrawled in faded marker. Rows of metal shelves lined one side, laden with forgotten personal items. Cobwebs stretched between the corners, and a single exposed bulb hung from the low ceiling, though it remained unlit.

Assuming since the lights were out in the hall, too, they were most likely alone, he shouted to the women, "Are you ladies alright?"

Renee calmed down enough to answer. She sniffed and croaked, "Yes."

Lavina also uttered an angry, "Yes," adding a few obscenities in Romani that Jet didn't understand.

Jet called out again, "Lavina, what do you think is happening?"

"My guess would be that Marik is in the middle of negotiations with Daria and Jack. We are the bargaining chips."

"So, what? They're holding us until he gets what he wants?" Renee's voice cracked as she screamed.

Lavina, ignoring Renee's rage, added calmly, "All we can do now is wait."

"For what?" Jet's voice was tight with frustration.

"Either they will give in to his demands, or he will have us killed. It is how it's done."

Renee began to sob again.

"Great!" Jet muttered as he shoved against the door once more, desperately searching for a way out.

Jet called out to Lavina again, "So, how did you get here? I thought you were going to the estate when you got off the plane?"

"We were taken at the airport, I presume much the same way you were brought here. Men in a van drove onto the tarmac and pulled us in."

"I don't understand; how did they know where we all were?"

"Giles is the only one absent from our group. I have always had my doubts about him and his loyalty. Now that Andrei is gone, I have had little use for him. I suspect he may have betrayed us to the Daniel clan. Perhaps they offered him a more suitable arrangement."

Jet took a few steps back and leaned against the closet's back wall. Figuring they would be there a while, he slid down the wall, the rough surface digging into his back as he lowered himself to the floor. He settled into the silence, his breathing the only sound in pitch-black that surrounded him.

Lavina, Renee, and Jet each sat, respectively, wondering if this was how Daria felt when she was taken the first time.

Lavina's mind drifted back over the last twenty years. She was more than just Daria's doctor and caregiver; she was her great-aunt, bound by blood and the complexities of family. Yet, that bond had been tainted by the circumstances of their relationship. How must Daria have felt, knowing that the woman who cared for her was also married to her kidnapper?

A pang of regret settled in Lavina's chest as she reflected on the role she had played—or failed to play—in Daria's life. She had done what she could within the constraints of her situation, but she knew it had not been enough. She had always been on the periphery, a distant figure when she should have been a guiding force.

As the darkness closed in around her, Lavina wondered if there was still a chance to make things right, now that Andrei was no longer controlling the situation. Maybe if they survived today, she could bridge the gap between them. Perhaps now they could find a way to reconcile.

Renee, the poor girl, was scared shitless. Her heart pounding in her chest, each beat a reminder of the uncertainty that now engulfed her. The recent news of her mother-in-law's abduction replayed in her mind, leaving her terrified for her own fate. Would she make it out alive? Would she ever see her new husband again?

This wasn't supposed to be her life. She was a farm kid from rural Kentucky, meant to be milking cows and riding her horses, not being kidnapped and used as a bargaining chip for some gangster gypsy, for God's sake.

Jet's emotions, however, were all over the place. Guilt still gnawing at him. He couldn't shake the feeling that he had failed Lily—failed to protect her from being taken—twice now. It was as if he was finally experiencing a fraction of what she must have gone through that fateful night, making him question if he somehow deserved what he was facing now.

Then, anger surged through him as he thought about his mother and uncle, the architects of his and Lily's fractured lives. They had stolen his son from him and the fury of it all brought an ache to his throat as a tear fell down his cheek.

But in the end, he knew how strong Lily had become, and then he rethought that introspection because Lily had always been the strong one. She was the one who stayed the course, who fought relentlessly for what she wanted, no matter the odds. And he knew she was out there right now, fighting for them. He had to remain strong, even if that was the only thing he could do for her, and for their son, right now.

His mind raced with Lily's words echoing in his head: *Stay alert, pay attention to your surroundings.* The irony of it all struck him. In the pitch-black room, 'surroundings' seemed like a distant concept. Suddenly, a light flickered on from under the door, and he heard Renee crying out again, followed a few moments later by gunshots in the distance.

He sprang to his feet, stumbling in the darkness as he moved toward the door. Pressing his ear against the cool metal, he strained to catch any sounds beyond his confinement. The muffled voices that followed made his heart race faster. He heard Lily's voice, fierce and urgent, calling out, "Jet! Renee!"

Pounding on the door, he shouted, "I'm here! I'm in here!"

Lily was at the door in an instant, her footsteps echoing in the hallway as she approached. She tried the handle, but a digital keypad held it locked. Frustration flared as she saw Jack's determined face; he attempted to kick in the door. It groaned under the force, but it didn't budge.

"Get away from the doors!" Lily shouted.

Jet's pulse pounded in his ears as he heard the sharp crack of Lily's gunshot. The sound reverberated off the metal door as the keypad sparked briefly before it swung open, revealing Jet's anxious face.

A second shot rang out. Renee's door flew open.

Stepping into the hallway, Jet's eyes adjusted as the third shot echoed down the corridor, and the metal door to Lavina's cell sprang open.

Lily quickly stepped aside, aiming her still smoking gun at the ceiling.

Lavina's security team leader, Viktor, stood at the front of the hall with two other members flanking each side. All of them had their weapons drawn and were surveying the chaos in the garage as party-goers fled the area.

Once Lily and Jack had everyone secured, they headed out. Using the chaos as cover, they weaved their way through the cars and out of the garage into waiting SUVs.

Jet and Lily were directed to the back seat of the first SUV while Jack, Renee, and Lavina boarded the second vehicle. As soon as the doors closed on the first SUV, the passenger shouted, "Let's move out!" They quickly merged into the flow of traffic.

Jet was the first to speak once they were sure they weren't being tailed. "What the hell happened back there?"

Lily made eye contact with the driver in the rearview mirror and said, "That's what I would call a perfect storm."

The driver said, "Mr. Thomas, we will debrief with our team leader when we get you back to the estate."

Jet nodded, accepting his answer, then turned his attention to Lily, putting his arm around her shoulder, pulling her in, and kissing the top of her head. "I knew you were a Badass."

She half laughed and looked up at him. He gave her his sexy, crooked smile, then took the opportunity to lean in and kiss her, leaving an "I love you" on her lips at the end.

Forty-five minutes later, evening had fallen, and they were back at the estate. Everyone involved settled into the studio for a debrief while the others stood watch around the grounds. Viktor called everyone to attention. "All right, everyone, settle in, and we'll get started." The rest of the team members sat and turned their attention to the front of the room. He began again, directing his attention to Lily. "Mrs. Stratton, could you start?"

"What do you need to know?"

"Can you give us an account of what took place starting from when you were taken by the van?"

"Well, just before that, I sat on the bench waiting for Jet. He came out of the studio, and we were going to walk around the property. I wanted to see the perimeter. We were headed onto the circular drive when a van pulled in. We figured it was more of the security team because they were in the same type of vehicle.

"We waited for them to park so we could direct them to the studio, but three hooded men jumped out and grabbed us when the doors opened. I fought with one of them, knocking him down. I pulled my weapon, and as he was trying to regain his strength, he came after me again, so I fired at him, hitting him in the leg. Then I fired at a fourth man holding the van door. I winged him on the shoulder. He fell back. I aimed my weapon at one of the men holding Jet and hadn't noticed the driver getting out of the vehicle. As I fired again, he tackled me to the ground, but they already had Jet in the van, and I was not going to leave him alone, so I dropped my weapon and let them take me, too.

Nodding. "We assumed as much from what we saw as we headed out of the building. We found your weapon on the ground." The second in command confirmed.

She continued, "They taped our hands and feet during the ride, and when we arrived at our destination, the back doors opened to a man smiling at us. He ordered them to free us."

"Did you know this man?" Viktor asked.

"No, not personally," she said, her voice firm but with a hint of sadness. "But I recognized him. It took a second, but his eyes ... he has the same eyes as Jet. Same as me ... same as Jack and Mum."

She glanced over at Jet, her expression full of regret. "I said his name, and he acknowledged it. It was my biological father, Marik Daniels.

"He told us to follow him, and he led us into this large room, which I assumed was the clubhouse or common area for the apartment complex we were at. A party was going on; I'm unsure if it was for us or if we were crashing someone else's, but he seemed to know the people.

"We were sitting at a table, and a few minutes later, they brought my son and his wife in, along with Lavina Marin. After they served us dinner, he asked Jack and me to follow him to somewhere quiet where we could talk.

"I hoped we would finally get some answers as to why we were abducted, so we went with him. He took us to an apartment on the fourth floor, claiming it was his cousin's.

"He started making small talk, but I asked him to cut to the chase. He then proceeded to tell us about our family history. About how our clan is tied to the Boswell clan, and how he met my mother. Then, how he had some issues with the King. He wanted our help and said he had a plan.

"His phone rang a couple of times, and he took the calls but walked out of the apartment for the second one. While we waited for him to return, Jack said he was uncomfortable with the situation."

"Actually, I said I didn't trust the mother—" He read the room and chose a more appropriate word. "Effer, and we needed to get the hell out of there."

Jet smiled at his son as Lily continued, "As I was saying, we felt uneasy. I stood up to glance outside and spotted a row of SUVs parked about a block away. I wasn't aware they belonged to us, so I advised Jack to grab something he could use as a weapon. He took a knife from the kitchen and sat back on the couch. Meanwhile, I positioned myself by the fireplace, near the poker. That's when I heard the door handle being turned.

"Marik came in smiling, saying it was time to focus on business. He emphasized our familial ties and how it connected us to his community. Repeating we were his heirs…"

Jack chimed in to say, "I asked him what exactly he had that I wanted, and he said the farm. Mom just about lost it. I thought she was gonna—"

"Anyway…" Glaring at Jack. "During our conversation, he said the eldest male owned all property in his culture, and that being him, he was the rightful owner of all the Stratton assets. He also noted that I had no right to own land or anything else as a clan woman and that any property I inherited would go to Jack after his passing."

"I told him I could make that happen for him."

"Jack! enough!"

"Okay, okay, sorry."

"Marik also declared that his plans were to manage any and all daily finances. Then he asserted we were to change the names of all banking and deeds so that he could allocate land for newcomers' housing and sell portions of land to satisfy the King. I told him in no uncertain terms that he was not to have anything to do with the farm and that if he thought my mother would not have put up with Romani culture, what made him think I would? Also, that his backward ways didn't work in America."

"Tell 'em what you really said, Mom." Jack snickered.

"At that point, he pulled out his phone and FaceTime'd someone walking down a hallway of doors. The man stopped and opened one of the doors, showing us Renee on the floor crying. Jack jumped up to attack Marik, but at that same moment, several men came crashing through the front door, grabbing Marik and us. Once they had us down in the garage, we could hear the gunfire. They pushed us down behind some cars and started yelling at each other in Romani. They took off with Marik, leaving us behind."

She pointed at one of the security team members. "That's when he came around the other side of the car and asked if we were okay. I said yes and that Jet and the others were being held in a hallway of doors. He said he knew where they were. He handed me a weapon and we headed in that direction. And ... well, you know the rest."

Jet spoke up, "I have some questions."

"Yes, Mr. Thomas?"

"First, how did you find us?"

Viktor turned to Lavina, who nodded in confirmation. He explained, "Mrs. Stratton has a tracking device implanted just beneath the skin at the back of her neck. It doesn't have GPS capabilities, but it allows us to detect her if we are within range. During the pursuit, we made the abductors believe they had lost us, but we were able to stay within range by tag teaming. Once we identified the vicinity, we could pinpoint her exact location."

"Wait!! You dog-chipped me?!"

"It's a little more sophisticated than that, but yes, ma'am."

"When?"

"On the plane the night they brought you to the US."

Lily glared at Lavina. "So, I never even had a chance, did I?"

Lavina responded, "You behave as if I had a choice in any of this. Marik's culture is my culture, too; my only rights were those Andrei allowed me to have. I knew nothing until you got Dr. Reed involved. Andrei needed someone he could trust to care for you after he got rid of him."

"What did he do to Doc!?" Lily demanded.

"Calm down, Daria, he did nothing to Doc. He told him you were a misbehaving and petulant child who lied about getting pregnant and claimed Levi wasn't the father to stir up trouble for the family. Doc quit!"

If that wasn't true, she thought. "And what about my grandfather's ear that you gave me as a punishment?" she demanded again.

"Of course, we did not cut off your grandfather's ear; it came from a corpse in the morgue I was working at."

"Jesus, Lavina! Are you even an actual doctor?"

"I am a coroner, but I hold a medical license."

Lily breathed deeply, relieved, as she finally understood what had happened to Doc and her grandfather. It was like a weight lifted, but it also shed light on why escaping had always been so impossible.

After a moment, she asked, "What about the phone numbers? How come all of my family and Jet's numbers were out of service?"

Jet spoke up, his voice carrying a mix of frustration and resignation. "I can answer that one. After you left—or rather, were taken—your family started getting prank phone calls. Mostly hang-ups, but some were mean-spirited, or so we thought at the time. Wallace said that they called and asked about you, claiming they knew where you were and that you were in danger. But Mum said they were lying because, at that point, the letters had started coming, telling us you were fine. So she suggested we all change our numbers. The family thought they gave you the new numbers in the letters they wrote back ... we believed her. Thinking back, it probably wasn't the best thing to do, but..." He shrugged, his expression showing the weight of hindsight and regret.

"Well, I guess I might have done the same if I were in my family's shoes. One last thing. Do we know what happened to Marik?" Lily asked.

Viktor answered, "When you and Mr. Thomas were taken, and Mrs. Marin didn't arrive with the rest of your family, I contacted an old associate of mine who now serves as one of the King's men for support since we are in their territory. King Alexei's son, Vano, was already searching for Marik as part of an investigation into the theft of tithes, along with accusations of extortion, unlawful seizures, and violent reprisals against those who couldn't pay. Mr. Daniels' cousin, who is loyal to the King, provided the King's men with Marik's location, and they were already en route to the apartment complex. We intercepted them a few blocks away and filled them in on the situation."

"What do you think they will do to him?" Daria asked.

Lavina answered, "Whatever it is, it won't be pleasant. "

Viktor reassured her, "Mrs. Stratton, you don't have to worry about seeing him again anytime soon. He will be serving at the King's leisure for many years to come. He's fortunate to come from royal lineage; otherwise, his fate would have ended in that garage. Instead, he'll face exile to one of the King's labor colonies—likely with a clan in the Jiu Valley—where he'll spend his days performing hard, menial work in the mines. His privileges will be stripped, and he'll live under constant supervision, a living reminder of the cost of betraying his own. Furthermore, his West Virginia clan now knows your family is under the protection of both the Marin clan and the King's men."

He then turned to Jack and said, "Mr. Stratton, I have a list of contacts in your area that you can reach out to if you ever need any assistance."

Jack nodded appreciatively. "Thanks. So, now what?"

Lavina walked over to Jack, gently taking his hand in hers and placing her other hand lovingly over it. "Let's get you home," she said softly.

Jet cleared his throat and added, "Actually, Lavina, his mother and I will handle getting them home. We'd like to spend some time with them before they have to get back to the farm."

Lavina glanced between Jet and Jack, understanding the sentiment. "Of course," she agreed, giving Jack's hand a reassuring squeeze.

Chapter Twenty-Four

Living in the Aftermath (2021)

The following day, Lavina and her security detail gathered their equipment and headed back to Romania, leaving Ana to help with Frank until Jet could find a suitable replacement.

Daria, Renee, and Ana were making dinner in Jet's kitchen while Jet and Jack talked in the studio. The conversation was light until Jet misspoke and called Jack, son.

Both men fell silent for a moment, the weight of the conversation hanging between them. Jet shifted slightly, trying to lighten the mood. "Well, that was awkward," he joked.

Jack chuckled, "Yeah, it's kind of funny. When I saw your name on my birth certificate, I was like, 'This can't be right, he's my cousin.' And now, I find out you're actually my father."

Jet nodded, a small smile playing at the corners of his mouth. "It's okay if things stay the same between us, you know? I get that I wasn't really present in your life as a father figure and that our relationship has been ... different."

"None of that was your fault, though," Jack replied.

Jet sighed, a mix of concern in his eyes. "Yeah, I know, but ... I just mean that however you see our relationship—whether it's more friendly or something else—is totally valid. For me, finding out you're my son gave me a new sense of belonging, like I finally had something truly mine. But it also felt like I was losing the past, the version of us I thought we had." He shrugged, offering Jack a sheepish look.

Jack nodded thoughtfully. "No, I get what you're saying. I felt that way at first too. It was a lot to take in, but now? I'm actually relieved to find out Levi Stratton wasn't my real dad. I never liked that guy. All the shit he put us through, especially mom. And then, finding out that one of my favorite people is actually my bio dad? That's pretty awesome. Losing a cousin doesn't seem like a big deal when I know I don't have any of that man's shitty traits in me. The only thing left is his name."

"I'd like to do something about that. I mean, if it's something you would be interested in."

"What do you mean?"

Jet's expression grew serious as he turned to face Jack more directly. His eyes spoke volumes—nervousness, hope, and a hint of excitement. Taking a deep breath, he spoke with careful deliberation.

"Two things," he began. "First, I want you to know how deeply I care for your mother. I've never felt this kind of connection with anyone before. When she left, I spiraled, Jack. I know, growing up, my behavior might've seemed off to you, so I'm sorry for any confusion or weirdness you saw. But just know, I was completely devastated."

Jet paused, glancing down for a moment before looking back at Jack with earnest eyes. "Since she came back, I'm finally starting to feel whole again. It's hard to explain, but it's like a piece of me was missing all those years, and now … it's like it's been put back in place. So, I'd be honored if you'd give me your blessing to ask her to marry me."

Jack stood still, processing the weight of Jet's words.

"Second," Jet continued, "I know you and I both believe that family is one of the most important things in life. That's why, when I found out I had a son, I had my attorney research the possibility of adopting you."

That caught Jack's attention, and Jet quickly explained, "I know you're over eighteen, and I know the UK has different laws, but I think this could bring us even closer as a family. It could also solve the name issue you and your mother seem to have."

With Jack still processing, Jet's voice took on a tone of quiet conviction. "Please, take your time to think it over. This process could take a while, and it might require a few trips back to the States for your mother and me. We're happy to do that, the more visits, the better as far as I'm concerned, but I want you to be sure before making any decisions. Talk to Renee about it too, because it will affect her as well. Whenever you're ready, let me know what you decide. No pressure."

"Whoa … dang, that was a lot to take in!" Jack half-laughed while crossing his arms and rolling his head back. He looked at his father and said, "Your first request is a total no-brainer, man. Of course, you've got my blessing. But aren't you still married to someone else?"

"It's just a matter of writing a check and signing a few more papers. It should be finalized in a couple of weeks."

"Does mom know?"

"I showed her the paperwork as soon as I got it."

"Well, it looks like you've covered your bases. Now you just gotta talk *her* into it."

Jet laughed out loud. "Yeah, that's the plan."

Jack walked over to his father and shook his hand firmly. Jet, with a grin, pulled him in for one of those bro hugs, as the door to the studio creaked open, and there stood Lily. She caught the tail end of their hug, pausing for a moment. Watching them, she felt a wave of relief and pride wash over her—her two men, finally connected in a way she had always hoped.

Satisfied and with a soft smile, she stepped inside. "Are you two boys ready for some dinner?" she asked.

Both men looked over at her and, as if on cue, they called out simultaneously, "I'm starving!"

Jack laughed. "Race you in, old man!"

Jet pretended to be offended and said, "Old? I can still beat your little ass."

"Oh, yeah?!"

They both took off running towards the door. Just before they reached it, Lily stepped out of their way. She watched them run towards the main house, pushing and trying to trip one another.

'Oh Lord, what am I going to do with these two?' She shook her head as she followed them. "Hey, play nice, you two!"

They turned back laughing as Jet shoved Jack to the side at the last second and was the first to enter through the door, winning the race. As the door closed, she could hear Jack saying, "Dude, I totally let you win!"

Jack and Renee stayed an additional week before they had to return to the farm. At the airport, Jet helped Jack and Renee settle on the private Marin charter.

"You sure about this, Jack? I mean, dropping the Stratton name—it's a big step," Jet said.

"I've never been more sure of anything. That name doesn't mean shit to me. You do. You and Uncle and even aunt Seebie and Frank have always been there, even when I didn't know the truth."

Jet smirked. "Well, let's make it official then. Just so you know, once you're adopted, no take-backs."

Jack laughed. "Wouldn't dream of it. Besides, it's about time I got a name that actually means something."

Renee joked, playfully nudging Jack. "You mean besides 'pain in the ass'?"

"Oh, that one's staying, Renee. Don't you worry." Jet chuckled.

Before they left, Jack helped his parents finish sorting through the remaining boxes. Many of their lingering questions found answers, and Jack was even able to fill in some gaps for his mother, sharing more about his experiences with Andrei and the other side of the family.

As they dug deeper into the past, Jack revealed some curious details. While sorting through boxes, Jack shared memories with his mother. Jack told her, "You're not gonna believe this, but when I was a kid visiting England, Uncle and Aunt Seebi paid me to pretend to be Andrei and Lavina's son."

Daria raised an eyebrow. "Wait, seriously? They paid you?"

Jack grinned. "Yeah, a small fortune—at least for a kid. I thought it was just a game, you know? As long as I got paid, I was happy to play along."

"And Romania? Did you get paid there too?"

Jack nodded, smiling. "Yep, even though that was evidently the truth."

"So, basically, you were a child actor with a very niche audience?"

Jack half laughed. "Guess you could say that. Uncle thought it showed my entrepreneurial spirit—said it was my 'Romani side coming through.'"

"Sounds about right."

"As I got older, though, I questioned his game. I guess Uncle realized he had to reveal at least some of the truth to keep me on board."

Andrei revealed Jack's heritage to him. Then warned him about the dangers of the Romani traveling lifestyle, emphasizing that their deep ethnic connections to other clans—ones less open to modern thinking—could put him and his mother in danger.

During several trips back to his homeland, Andrei showed Jack some of the harsh realities of Romani life: the poverty and racism his people endured.

In the shadowed alleys of forgotten lands, many Roma lived in isolated slums where electricity and running water were a distant memory. There, amid crumbling walls and makeshift shelters, they fought a daily battle for survival, fraught with hardship and uncertainty.

Denied even the most basic human rights, they navigated a world where access to healthcare was a luxury reserved for the privileged. Instead, they faced illness and injury with little hope of aid.

The threat of forced evictions loomed daily as municipalities and landowners tore down their homes, often leaving them with nothing but the clothes on their backs and the weight of despair in their hearts.

The ever-present figures of authority cast a shroud of fear over their already precarious existence, their heavy-handed tactics a constant reminder of their vulnerability. Yet, despite the darkness, a flame of resilience flickered—a testament to the unconquerable spirit of the Roma people.

Andrei fiercely held on to this spirit, and despite their trials, they persevered, finding solace in the bonds of community and the strength of tradition.

One day, after taking Jack through a Romanian slum, Uncle asked, "Is this what you want for you and your mother? Never knowing where your next meal would come from? Never having a permanent place to lay your head at night? Because if you were to be brought back here, this would be your life. Does this look like the future you want for yourself?"

"No, sir!" Jack insisted. "I want to stay on the farm."

Andrei knew that, as American citizens, Jack and Daria enjoyed certain freedoms that they would be unwilling to forgo and he knew Jack was now old enough to understand them, too. "Good, I hoped you would feel that way. This is why it is important for you to keep our little secret. Not only for your safety but for your mothers safety, too. She is unaware of the dangers that may befall her if she were to return to her homeland."

Jack promised Uncle he would never reveal his secret, desperately wanting to ensure the safety and way of life for his mother and extended family.

But Andrei withheld crucial information, particularly about Jack's parentage. Though Jack learned about his and his mother's Romani ethnicity, Andrei never disclosed which specific lineage she belonged to or its significance. Nor did he reveal Levi was not Jack's father, or that Levi had been chosen for that role due to a deal Andrei had made with a West Virginia judge. Jack only discovered this through his mother and additional records found in the boxes.

Based on Andrei's journal entries, Daria's impression of him proved accurate. While not a Rom Baro, Andrei was a highly respected elder in his community, facilitating many agreements with local authorities that benefited the local clans in the States and his homeland.

As it turned out, Levi was the son of a prominent beef cattle rancher of Irish Traveler descent from northern West Virginia and a county commissioner. His father needed to keep Levi out of jail during an election cycle. Andrei needed a man to play the role of husband to his unwed and possibly pregnant great-niece at the time, along with handling various other favors for local clansmen's misdeeds. Through bribes and backroom promises, the three parties arranged a deal to take Levi and Daria out of state to Kentucky, change their identities, and set them up somewhere secluded.

The original property was about twenty miles from any populated area or town. Although Andrei had originally bought and paid for it for another Romani family, Levi's father repaid the cost and, wanting nothing more to do with him, he specifically requested a no-contact arrangement.

The properties surrounding the little homestead were eventually bought with money Jet had given to his mother from royalties and record sales to help them live a better life. She, in turn, gave a portion of it to Andrei to help subsidize Levi and Daria's homestead. What wasn't used was invested in Jack's future.

After examining the bank transactions and records found in Daria's file box, Jet could at least find some solace in his mother's actions.

Even though he remained thoroughly convinced that her actions were unnecessary, considering that the Daniel Clan eventually found Daria and Jack anyway, he appreciated the fact that she had provided for her grandson.

Now that Jet had delivered the kids to the airport and helped them settle on the private Marin charter, he drove back to his estate.

When Jet returned, Lily was nowhere to be found. Concerned, he accessed his security network and saw her packing her bags through the cameras. He understood she had a business to run nearby and needed to ensure Sully's return to retirement, but a wave of disappointment washed over him. He had hoped she would stay at the estate so they could spend some quality time alone and reconnect. Even though he knew where she would be, the prospect of being apart left him feeling empty and alone once again.

After spending a week bonding with his son, getting to know his new daughter-in-law, and having his whole family together under one roof, he now felt more ready than ever to fully commit to this woman. But now, Jack's words echoed in his mind—was he really going to have to talk her into it?

Jet wasn't going to take any chances, letting her get comfortable back in her little studio. He wanted her with him, so he grabbed his coat and headed to the pub.

He sat at his usual booth, chatting with locals, watching her work, and waiting for the pub to close. Her ability to connect with people was unmistakable in every interaction. Customers felt not only welcomed but truly at home in her presence. Sully had made the right decision in hiring her. She was a natural, and as the new owner, Jet had reaped the benefits of her talents. Although he had planned to give the pub to her as a wedding present, he realized that, regardless of her response to his proposal, it deservedly belonged to her.

He continued watching her, reflecting on their convoluted dance with fate. It struck him as curious how certain individuals, even people who lived worlds apart, could enter our lives with a purpose, arriving at just the right moment. It had happened to them all those years ago, and now, destiny or fate or the stars had once again brought them together.

He thought about their recent conversations, especially the one about her fear of loss, and now the weight of her fears fell heavily on his mind, as they had become his fears, too. The memory of his own deep-rooted anguish flooded back. The thought of experiencing that kind of loss again was stifling, and remembering the distress etched on her face during their talk only solidified his belief that he would most certainly have to talk her into it.

When the time came for her to ring for last drinks, Jet helped Lily close up. He told the other employees they could leave early, and they worked quietly together. When Jet walked the last straggler to the door and said goodnight, he locked it and went to find Lily. She was in the kitchen, stacking the last of the plates. He stood at the entrance, watching her.

She caught him staring. "What?"

"Oh, nothing." He sauntered over to her and pulled her in for a long kiss.

"Mmm, what was that for?" she asked, slightly breathless.

"A thank you."

"For what?"

"For coming home."

She pulled away from him, noticing the subtle shifts in his expression. He seemed serious, not playful as she had expected. She leaned back, searching his eyes, her senses now attuned to the urgency in his voice. "What's going on, babe?"

"I want you to come home with me."

"Tonight?"

"Every night."

"Jet," she sighed, "I think we need to slow down a bit."

"Lil, I know you're afraid of moving too fast and something happening again, but we're safe now. We know who to call if anything happens. The kids have their people to call. Marik is out of the picture, with the King holding him in servitude, and his clan is being watched. Hell, I have my own little badass right here in town."

She rolled her eyes at him.

"Besides, with all the security I've installed, it would be safer for you at the estate, anyway."

"What about the sleeping arrangements?" she asked, knowing it was a silly question. They had already been intimate since her return, and Jet was right about everyone being safe now. But something kept pricking the back of her mind, nudging her away from this man. Was it just the fear of being torn apart again, as he suggested, or something else?

He pulled her close again. "We can keep the sleeping arrangements like we did when the kids were here. Hell, you can even have your own wing if you want ... or you can keep me company in my bed." He wriggled his eyebrows at her.

She half laughed and shook her head. "Lily, I meant what I said; I don't want you out of my sight ever again. Trust me, I know how that sounds, but I think we need this. I think we owe it to ourselves to take this chance to be together again. Don't you?"

And there it was. The pricking in her mind came full circle to scream at her ... It wasn't fear at all. Everything he said was true. They were safe. The kids were safe. She knew who to call and how to take care of herself. So, what was it?

The realization hit her like a slap—the loss of independence. How ridiculous was that? But in hindsight, it was something she had grown quite accustomed to. Ever since she was taken, she had truly been on her own. There was no one she could trust, and when Jack came, ensuring his safety and caring for him became her number one priority. With precious little help. And with the isolation of her farm, there was no one to turn to.

It had become her way of life, her safety blanket. She was the only person she could count on. The only person she trusted. Now, the thought of living under someone else's roof, being taken care of by someone else, and being accountable to someone else. Could she even do it? Did she even *want* to do it?

As a young woman, that's *all* she wanted—for him to love her, protect her, and be with her in every way. She never wanted to leave his side. And now, what was the old saying about putting childish things away? But then, what was all this for if it wasn't to be together again? She didn't fight, dream, and come all this way just to be alone, did she?

"Lil?" He pulled her from her thoughts. "Hey, where'd you go?"

She sighed, holding her answer. And just as she was about to say something, Jet blurted out, "Lily, I want you to marry me. I want us to spend the rest of our lives together as that old married couple Pops always accused us of being. I want to make up for lost time and fuck like teenagers again. I want to wake up next to you every day, no matter where we are, and see your beautiful eyes looking back at me. I want you to rip me a new one every time I fuck up. Jesus, Lil, we are in the prime of our lives, and I don't want to spend one more second away from you. And when we're old, I want to sit on a porch in Kentucky and watch our grandchildren. And—"

"Okay, okay, I get the picture!" She laughed as he furiously attacked her lips, then slowed to speak between kisses.

"Is that ... a yes?"

"Yes ... of course, it's yes ... it's always been yes. Oh God, I'm gonna regret this, aren't I."

"Absolutely..."

Chapter Twenty-Five

Epilogue

(2022) Six months later ...

The day was like any other—or so Lily thought. The mid-morning sun streamed through the windows of the pub, casting a golden glow over the old wooden tables. Lily wiped down the bar, lost in the rhythm of her work, when her phone buzzed with a call from Jet.

"Hey, love," Jet's voice crackled through the line, a hint of urgency beneath his usual calm tone. "I need you to come home. We've got a bit of an emergency here at the manor."

Lily's heart skipped a beat, worry flickering in her chest. "An emergency? What happened? Are you okay?"

"Just come home, Lil. I'll explain when you get here," Jet said, his voice firm but reassuring.

She wasted no time putting one of the employees in charge as she grabbed her things and dashed out the door. Lily drove straight to the manor, her mind racing with all the plausible scenarios. What could be wrong? Has something happened to Jet? Her nerves were frayed by the time she pulled up the gravel drive.

But when she stepped inside, expecting chaos, she was met with something different. Penny stood in the entryway, a knowing smile on her face and a glimmer in her eyes.

"Penny? What's going on? Where's Jet?" Lily asked, her voice laced with confusion.

Penny took her by the hand, leading her up the stairs. "Come on, love, let's get you ready."

"Ready for what?" Lily's confusion only deepened, but Penny just chuckled, guiding her into a room where a beautiful dress hung waiting.

"Penny, what's all this? Why do I need to get ready?"

Penny grinned, mischief in her eyes. "It's your wedding day, sweetie!"

Lily's jaw dropped. "What? No ... we haven't even talked about a date yet."

"Well, someone has been planning this for a couple of months now." Penny raised her hand over her head, pointing to herself.

"Wait a minute. Does Jet know about this?"

"Who do you think asked me to plan it, silly?" Penny handed Lily a flute of champagne. "Drink up. You're getting married today!"

Lily took a big gulp, her mind still reeling. "This is crazy. I mean, I love it, but—what if I wasn't ready? What if I said no?"

Penny raised an eyebrow. "But you're not going to say no, though, are you?"

Lily sighed, shaking her head with a smile. "Of course not. It's just—Jet and his surprises. He never does anything half-assed, does he?"

"Not when it comes to you," Penny said, giving her a wink.

At this point, Lily found herself following Penny's lead, her mind still reeling as she tried to process everything. Penny motioned for her to come closer, gently helping her out of her clothes and into the new dress. As Lily went along with it, the realization began to settle in—this wasn't an emergency—this was something far more sinister. This was an ambush! She eyed Penny with furrowed brows.

"Seriously, Penny. You and Jet—you guys are too much. I can't believe you pulled this off without me finding out."

Penny just smiled. "We wanted it to be perfect for you, Lil."

Still confused, she protested, but Penny shushed her. "Relax!" She continued to apply Lily's make-up. "It seems to me we've done this before," Penny mused, with a twinkle in her eye. "Remember? Me helping you with your makeup on my wedding day?"

Lily laughed, the tension melting away as she recalled the memory. "I do. I also remember the girls had to redo your eyeliner three times because you kept crying. Oh my gosh, this is insane. Is this really happening? I mean a real wedding?"

Penny grinned, stepping back to admire her handiwork. "Yes, this is happening. A real wedding! Only this time, it's yours."

When Lily was ready, Penny led her downstairs to the backyard, where a small gathering awaited her. Family and close friends stood around, their faces beaming with love and happiness. She barely noticed the tears brimming in her eyes until she saw the bouquet Penny had put in her hands—wildflowers and grasses, arranged just like the ones she used to pick from the park down the street from their childhood homes. It was perfect.

As Lily passed each familiar face, her heart swelled. Aunt Minnie was there, her gentle smile radiating warmth, along with her son Jack and daughter-in-law Renee, who waved with excitement. Jet's father, Frank, stood tall and proud, a glimmer of emotion in his eyes. Sully and Fi exchanged knowing looks, and Ronny and Penny shared an arm-in-arm moment, both looking thrilled. Reggie stood off to the side, charming as ever, accompanied by his latest muse of the month. Even Lavina had come, her presence a testament to her ongoing effort to mend the ties strained by the past. Slowly, Lily was beginning to accept her into the family.

Jet stood at the end of the aisle, looking impossibly handsome, his expression a mix of adoration and awe. His eyes locked on hers as if she were the only person in the world. She took a shaky breath, her emotions threatening to overwhelm her, as she walked toward him, step by step, toward the future they were about to begin together.

"Hey," she whispered as she reached him, her voice trembling with emotion.

"Hey," Jet replied, squeezing her hands. "You look beautiful, Lil. Just like I imagined."

"Nice touch with the flowers. They're perfect," she whispered.

Jet smiled, taking her hands in his. "I remembered you saying you wanted a pretty dress and a bouquet just like the ones you picked that day you told me we were getting married. Took a little longer than expected but ...." He shrugged, a playful glint in his eyes. "I wanted this to be everything you dreamed of." He paused, his gaze softening as he looked into her eyes. "I couldn't wait any longer to call you my wife. And—well, didn't want to take the chance of you changing your mind."

Lily laughed softly, tears spilling down her cheeks. "I would never change my mind."

The officiant cleared his throat, and the ceremony began. At the point they were to exchange vows, Jet spoke up and said he wanted to say something.

"Lily, from the moment you walked into my life, you turned my world upside down in the best way possible. I was never one to believe in fate, but with you, I've come to realize that some things are meant to be. You've taught me patience, trust, and what it truly means to love unconditionally.

"I promise to stand by you through every high and every low, to be your rock when the world feels unsteady, and to be your biggest supporter in everything you do. I vow to cherish you, to laugh with you, to hold you close on stormy nights, and to dance with you when the sun shines.

"You are my best friend, Lil. My confidant, and the love of my life. Today, I commit to you completely, my heart and my soul. Please know that whatever life throws our way, we'll face it together, you and me, hand in hand. I love you—for now and always."

Jet's heartfelt vows caught Lily off guard. She smiled, a mix of tears and laughter bubbling up as she looked into Jet's eyes.

"Jet," she began, her voice soft and trembling. "I didn't know you were going to do this, and I don't have anything written down. But I know how much I love you, how much you mean to me. So, I guess I'll just speak from my heart."

She took a deep breath, her hands gripping his. "You've always been my anchor, my safe place, even when you didn't realize it. You've seen me at my best and my worst, and yet you stand here, choosing me, loving me. I can't promise perfect words or a perfect life, but I can promise you this—I'll love you with everything I have, every day for the rest of my life. I'll be by your side, no matter what comes our way. You're my home, Jet, and there's nowhere else I'd rather be."

Lily paused, a tear slipping down her cheek. "So, I guess these are my vows to you. I vow to keep surprising you, to keep loving you, and to always choose you—just like you've chosen me."

Then the officiant finally said, "Well, I guess my job here is done, John you may kiss your bride," Jet pulled Lily into a deep, passionate kiss that left them both breathless. As they pulled apart, Jet grinned, elated.

"Welcome home, Mrs. Thomas," he whispered, his voice full of love.

Lily smiled up at him, feeling a sense of completeness she'd never known before. "Home," she echoed, knowing that wherever Jet was, that's exactly where she belonged.

As they turned to face their loved ones, the crowd erupted in cheers and applause. Lily couldn't help but feel that this was the beginning of a beautiful new chapter in their lives. Jet had ensured every detail of the day was perfect—and in that moment, she knew the best was yet to come.

Chapter Twenty-Six

(2045)

Letter to the reader

J et and I are visiting the kids this week and as I sit on the porch swing of Jack's farmhouse—the one he and Renee built on the site of the old cabin—sipping my iced tea, I can't help but reflect on our lives. The echoes of old memories have faded, now replaced by the warmth of new ones that continue to be made. It's funny, ya know, how time seems to do that—change things and give new perspectives. The heartache this place once brought has now been replaced with pride and joy. What was once a prison to me is now a thriving dairy operation. Jack and Renee have turned it into something truly remarkable.

Our three grandchildren are grown now. John, the eldest, along with Sarah-Jane and Michael, have each found their own paths in the world. John, with his strong work ethic and deep connection to the land, chose to stay close to his roots. It fills my heart with pride that he decided to work alongside his father, creating a family legacy. There's something special about seeing them together, building upon what was started so many years ago. The same land that once felt like a burden now thrives under their care, and I can see the future in every new idea John brings to the table.

As for me, I sold Sully's a while back to a young Irish couple. They had become regulars over the years, and it was clear they'd fallen in love with the place, just like I did. They reminded me so much of a young Sully and Fi—the same energy, passion, and unbreakable bond. I knew in my heart they were the right ones to take over.

Letting go wasn't easy. Sully's had been my refuge, my sanctuary, and the place where so many of our stories were written. It's strange not being there every day, not seeing the familiar faces or hearing the clink of glasses as the day's first customers came through the door. But it was time. Time for someone else to carry on the traditions, to breathe new life into the old place.

I've heard they've done well with it. They've made some changes, of course—put their own stamp on it—but the spirit of Sully's remains. I sometimes think about dropping by, just to see how it's faring under their care. But then I remind myself that it's their turn now, just as it was mine when Sully passed the torch. It's comforting, in a way, knowing that his legacy will continue, that the laughter and stories will live on, even if I'm not the one behind the bar anymore.

And then there's Jet—my rock, my love. Who would have thought that the boy who flounced down in front of me when I was just six years old would end up becoming my forever? His journey has been incredible. Two Grammys now sit proudly on our mantle, and five years ago, the band was inducted into the Rock & Roll Hall of Fame. It was a moment of immense pride, not just for him, but for all of us who supported him along the way. He doesn't tour as much these days, but when he does, the energy and passion he brings to the stage are still unmatched. Watching him perform still gives me the same thrill it did when we were younger.

At home, he's still the same Jet I fell in love with—kind, funny, and always ready with that crooked grin that never fails to make me weak. Despite the fame and all the accolades, he's managed to find a balance between his music and our life together, something we both needed more than anything. We've weathered countless storms, faced our share of challenges, but through it all, we've come out stronger. And here we are—still standing, still strong, and still deeply in love. Every day with him still feels like a gift, and I wouldn't trade it for the world.

Now, as the sun sets over the fields of our lives, casting a golden glow on everything we've built, I realized, long ago, that life is full of twists and turns, of pain and joy—and all of it is worth remembering. That's why I've put pen to paper to share our stories. A sort of tribute to the resilience of the human spirit. I want you to know that even when life takes you down an unexpected path, there's always hope waiting on the other side. Believe it or not, Uncle helped me hold on to mine ... at a time when I was at my lowest and had resigned myself to the life that was chosen for me. He reminded me I was still capable of love and hope. I still have the note.

By sharing our journey, I hope you find your own sense of hope, inspiration, or maybe even a small piece of yourself in the pages of our lives. After all, we're all just trying to find our way, and sometimes it helps to know that someone else has been there, too.

As you walk your own path, whether in quiet reflection or bold steps forward, may you discover the peace you seek, or at least a glimmer of hope to guide you through uncertainty. Life's journey isn't always easy, and the road ahead may be winding, but remember—every twist, every turn is part of your story. Embrace it, learn from it, and keep moving forward. There's strength in knowing you're not alone, and that peace, however elusive, is always worth pursuing.

Daria M. Thomas